ARMS
of an
Angel

*Linda Boulanger*

# Arms of an Angel
By Linda Boulanger

Cover Design: Tell~Tale Book Covers
Published by: TreasureLine Publishing

www.LindaBoulangerBooks.com

Also available in eBook publication

PRINTED IN THE UNITED STATES OF AMERICA

*There are people who will cross your path*
*that'll change the course for the good or bad.*
*Those who change it for the better—*
*Those are the people I call angels.*
*Perhaps earthly angels of sorts...*

Perhaps we all play the part of an
earthly angel at some point in our lives...
Perhaps we should check for our wings.

Author's Note

A cover change for *Arms of an Angel* offered me the
opportunity to revamp the inside as well. Whether you've
met Claire and Garrett before or this is your first time
indulging in their story, I hope you'll enjoy this revised
edition. Grab some tissues, and be sure to let me know if
you end up using them. *~Linda*

.

*Sometimes it's hard to tell where one*
*set of wings ends and the other begins...*

Claire wasn't exactly the type of girl a guy would normally choose to take home to meet his mamma. Yet there she was, on her way to meet Garrett's parents. Her heart slammed against her chest, hidden in part by the sweetheart neckline of her blue Carin Morrow. It was the most modest dress she owned and it still showed an ample amount of flesh. She'd tried to cover a bit more with a simple sweater, but wasn't at all sure if she'd been successful. Her wardrobe had been purchased to enhance and show off her assets, not hide them. Dressing to meet parents was not a priority... at least it hadn't been until now. And on such short notice... She still simmered at Garrett's demand that she get out of bed and get ready to go to his parents' farm. The man had no right to tell her what to do. Hell, he had no right to have barged into her apartment in the first place.

Yet there she was, sitting in the passenger seat of his car, teetering between anger and disbelief -- all of it mixed with fear. She was sure Garrett's parents would see right through her. The thought of their disapproving faces filled her with an even greater sense of dread. She wasn't fit for any man, let alone one as virtuous as Garrett. He was her angel. He'd saved her, yet she didn't deserve him. He certainly didn't deserve to be saddled with a woman like her.

Claire leaned back against the seat, her mind

wandering as the passing view changed from steel and concrete to green hills and pastures.

Unwise decisions. That's what Claire seemed best at making. Incidents in her own life were what she'd chosen to blame - two to be more precise. She'd lost her parents in a car accident and battled cancer, both at the sweet age of nineteen. Not only had she found herself alone, the cancer had left her without the body parts to ever carry her own child, furthering her sense of being forsaken and useless.

For four years she'd dived into one indulgence after another in an attempt to make the hurt inside subside. Fast men and free flowing liquor had been her choice as she'd commenced to working hard at partying through her inheritance, though nothing seemed to work. Oh, she'd come close a time or two. On occasion, her senses numbed to where she felt little more than a dull ache, but the piercing pain always returned after too short a time. Hope vanished as did her desire to go on. She'd decided life was no longer worth living.

And that's the point where Garrett had come into her life....

# Chapter 1

Claire could feel him watching her in the mirror, knew his eyes were assessing her, undressing her. She didn't mind. Knowing men desired her made her feel alive, worthwhile... most of the time.

Ranauld looked away as she turned to face the front of the limousine, though his gaze returned as soon as he realized her focus was not on him. She was pensive - an unusual disposition for this particular client. He smiled. Unusual was the perfect word to describe her, regardless of her mood. Of all his filthy rich, high society clients, no one could compare to Claire Orion. Of course, there weren't many who had allowed him the liberties she had, either. None, actually. The thought of their last encounter ramped up his always-present desire for her. He frowned. She had to know he was hungry, yet she wasn't biting, even though he'd tried to engage her several times throughout her afternoon shopping spree. He wondered what had captured her. She was definitely a woman looking within.

Claire moved from his line of vision as she leaned toward the passenger side window. The driver couldn't see the look of pain that pulled her finely arched brows toward her beautiful blue-gray eyes. He didn't see her hand press against the tinted window as she watched a little girl walking hand in hand with her father. He didn't know Claire well enough to know how much she'd yearned for acceptance from her own father or how it had affected the woman she had become. Ranauld, like most, only knew the larger than life persona in the pretty little package that his passenger most often presented to the world. There were few with even an inkling of a notion that beneath her flawless exterior lay a woman with scars she believed incapable of healing.

Ranauld missed Claire's heavy sigh as he focused his attention on the circle drive in front of her historic building. With the ease of a man used to handling the large vehicle, he maneuvered through the traffic and pulled to a stop outside the double doors. By the time he opened the door for her, Claire had masked her bitterness. Her father was gone. There'd been no one to bridge the gap between them; no one he respected enough that was willing to step in to help.

"Perhaps I can be of service to you later, Ms. Orion? I could make arrangements to see that you make it home safely this evening." Ranauld's eyes begged as he helped her from the limousine.

Claire smiled in that mischievous way that made her nose crinkle; the one that should have alerted a man he was about to be toyed with. "Why, Mr. Ranauld, I'm afraid you've made a dreadful error. I can't imagine what would make you think I'm planning to go out?"

"My apologies for the assumption. I was thinking of your shopping, the packages. They usually accompany an evening out." He continued to fish. "So you'll be home? Alone?"

"I didn't say that." She knew what he wanted. He knew she knew. She ran her hands through her dyed blonde hair in a way that reminded Ranauld of how it felt to have his hands entwined in the soft lushness of her beautiful curls. Her eyes danced as she moistened her lips with the tip of her tongue before continuing. "But... I've got your number.

I'll call if the need arises. A woman can't be too careful about who she lets take her home, or who she lets stay…"

The building doorman chuckled as he held the door for her before retrieving her packages from the wilting chauffer. "Perk up, man." The older gent clapped Ranauld on the back as he took Claire's bags. "She's got your number."

Charlie went away laughing, wondering how many other hearts were hurting over the unpossessable Claire Orion. He wasn't sure if that was a word even. What he did know was that Claire Orion was her own woman. The only man who'd ever had a hold on her had been her father and he'd never given her an ounce of anything except heartache. He snorted, thinking of the number of times she'd left the building crying over something he knew that man had said to her. A quick death behind the wheel of a car was too good for him. It was far better than he deserved after the way he'd killed Claire's dreams and sense of worth. It was more than he'd given his daughter who had been dying inside for a good many years.

Charlie could only hope she'd live long enough to learn to believe in herself. She was a beautiful woman with a heart of gold and a generosity to match, but the way she lived… He shook his head and looked up toward the heavens. Claire needed to find her place in this world. She needed someone to help her, and fast.

# Chapter 2

Claire caressed the bottle of pills, a wave of euphoria washing over her as she placed them on her nightstand and patiently dressed, taking great pains with every detail of her appearance. She wanted this last meal to be special. She wanted all eyes at the restaurant to be on her. She wanted to look spectacular when she was found.

Her mouth watered as she thought of the titillating array of scrumptious delicacies that awaited her with her last minute reservation at the extravagant Minuet. It had surprised Claire that she was able to get in on such short notice, but when she'd called in and the Maitre d' had taken her name, he'd assured her that she need not worry.

"I've got it right here. Check and double check," he'd told her.

Claire had decided it was an omen. The meal was to be the beginning of her end. She smiled as she went down to meet the cab Charlie had called for her. She hadn't wanted Ranauld returning – hadn't actually desired his services earlier in the day either, though a cancellation by Mr. Donovan in 3C had placed him at her disposal.

She arrived at the restaurant dressed in her finest. Black Fuarento cocktail dress straight from the runways of Italy, black lace hose, black designer heels in the latest French fashion. Heads turned as she walked by. Claire Orion looked good and she knew it.

"Table for Orion." She flashed her most disarming smile at the man whose eyes shone with recognition and admiration.

"Check and double check," he said, and they both laughed quietly before he asked if she'd like to go ahead to her table.

"Hmm." Claire ran a painted nail across her lips bringing attention to their fullness as she flirted with the Maitre d'. "If I'm to eat, I shall need to sit, and preferably at one of your finely set tables." She trailed the same finger along the buttons of his tailored jacket causing his voice to catch as he answered her. Claire smiled as he offered her his arm.

"Away we go then, my lady." Claire slipped her hand into the crook of his arm and he escorted her to a cozy table toward the back of the restaurant.

"Perfect!"

Oh how Claire loved the fineries of life. If only she could enjoy them with out the pain, she thought as she ordered appetizers and wine: calamari, sautéed zucchini, and a fine Chateau Lafite-Rothschild - the best money could buy. Sitting back, she scrutinized the occupants of the other tables as she waited for her hors d'oeuvres. People watching without seeming overtly rude and obvious -- it was a pastime she'd managed to perfect through the years of being hauled from one boring event to another at the side of one or both of her parents.

An older couple sat nearby holding hands across the table. An anniversary, perhaps, Claire thought with a smile as she watched the gentleman bring his love's aged fingers to his lips. Regret nudged. There'd be no such love for her. Who'd want her? What good was a woman who couldn't have children? She was good for one thing only and Claire was quickly growing tired of the revolving door of partners who offered little more than momentary diversion. She'd have loved to have found one who looked at her, even for a moment, the way the older gentleman was looking at his wife. But the ones she'd been with were all the same. They cared only for what she could offer them at the moment she was with them.

Claire shrugged. *C'est la vie* - such was life. And for Claire, it was over. She returned to the people around her, finding one level down and several tables over, a group of business colleagues discussing strategies, their hard driving boss, and their annoying counterparts in various companies and even within competing groups within their own organization. Claire was thankful she'd been well provided for and able to avoid the doldrums and politics of the work-a-day world.

She had just turned her attention to another table where a man sat with two women when Anthony, as her waiter had introduced himself earlier, returned with her pre-meal delicacies. She smiled knowing he was appreciating the view, leaning toward her just a bit more than he needed as he placed her platters and filled her wine glass.

"Thank you, Anthony. Perhaps you should consider returning a thank you to me as well." Claire laughed as the man's cheeks burned and he realized he'd been caught.

"I'm so sorry…" He wrestled with the words of his apology. Undoubtedly he could see his tip and perhaps even his job disappearing.

Claire winked at him. "No harm. This dress was made for appreciation, wouldn't you think? Only, you might consider being a bit more discreet in the future. As I'm sure you're aware, some women would find your attention flattering. Others… not so much. There are those who will make a scene merely because they can." He nodded and smiled graciously before he thanked her and walked away.

Claire turned her attention back to the other table as

she tasted the calamari. Splendid, she thought. The eyes of the man at the table with the two women echoed that thought about her. Claire had indeed succeeded at one thing in life: making herself desirable. It was all a woman like her could be. Without the ability to give a man children, she'd be nothing but a playmate; certainly not a proper wife.

The woman on the opposite side of the table from Claire's admirer suddenly realized he was flirting with someone besides her friend. She glared at Claire and then the man before kicking him under the table. Claire could not suppress quiet laughter as his flirtations turned to painful surprise. She shrugged her bare shoulders and smiled as the woman again looked at her and shook her head as if it was all Claire's fault. Perhaps his female counterpart should try being less talkative and more attentive to her own appearance. He braved another glance in Claire's direction as his date's friend busied herself with finding something in her bag. Claire pretended to drop her napkin and leaned over to retrieve it. She may as well make his risk worthwhile.

As she righted herself, her attention was captured by the Maitre d' chattering away to a rather attractive gentleman as they neared her table. She'd missed his hasty, breathless arrival, had no idea how he'd had to rush to get there, late as usual. She had a bird's eye view of the surprise that contorted his handsome face when the Maitre d' told him his date had already arrived, though.

"You're a lucky man, Mr. O'Bryan, to have such a lovely wife."

They stopped beside Claire's table. Garrett's brows dipped. Claire stared up at the two men in confusion. The Maitre d' smiled.

"Is there a problem?" Claire asked, though her words

were partially covered over by Garrett's voice.

"Wife?" he whispered, then added, "I'm not married."

Now the other man's face registered confusion. He looked from Garrett to Claire and back again.

"You're sure she's not your wife?" he asked, his mouth lifting at the corners in a tentative, hopeful smile. Garrett shook his head. "O'Bryan?" He turned back to Claire in despair. She shook her head.

"Orion," she answered trying hard to suppress her mirth. It was obvious now why she'd gotten a table so easily.

The Maitre d' closed his eyes, undoubtedly shuffling through options. It was clear the house was packed with no available tables. His musings were interrupted by Garrett's cell phone.

"Donna? Where are you?" Garrett asked the unseen. "Oh. Right. I'm sorry to hear that. Okay. Yes. Another time, perhaps. Well, if she's still ill, of course you must stay and take care of her. Good-bye." He placed the phone back in his pocket then looked at the two sets of eyes that watched and waited.

"Well, Mr. Ballard. It looks like it's your lucky evening. My date has had to cancel. I won't need my table after all."

Obvious relief washed over Mr. Ballard's face.

"I'm sorry to have interrupted your evening, Ms. Orion." Garrett nodded to her then turned to leave.

"Mr. O'Bryan?" she called, the caress of her voice causing him to turn back. He raised his brows in answer and waited. "Since you're already here and undoubtedly haven't eaten yet, would you care to join me? My treat. It's the least I could do for taking your table."

Garrett studied the beautiful woman while he

contemplated her proposal. He felt eyes on him from all directions and knew there wasn't a man in the place that didn't wish he was in Garrett's shoes.

"Well?" she smiled. She knew it too.

"I'd love to." He returned to the table. "And, you're right. I'm starving." He slipped into the seat across from her.

"Perfect. Will you have a glass of wine or shall we request a bottle of champagne to add to the conversational fodder?" she asked in her most conspiratorial tone. He glanced around noting how eyes quickly turned away.

"Oh champagne , of course. We can toast our unique beginning..." he played along and she clapped quietly.

"You heard the gentleman, Mr. Ballard. Bring out the finest. And quickly before the magical moment passes by."

"Of course! And on the house," the Maitre d' told her. Turning, he snapped his fingers and rushed away.

"Our meal will be free as well, no doubt. Oh don't worry," she said when the man sitting across from her raised his brows. "I'll leave a tip that will more than make up for whatever might come out of our dear Mr. Ballard's own pocket." Claire laughed freely.

"I hardly know you and I'd already say I'm correct in guessing you have quite the ornery streak in you." Garrett shook his head though the corners of his mouth curved upward.

"His was an honest mistake, I suppose. Though these shenanigans have caused my hors d'oeuvres to grow cold. You wouldn't mind skipping right to the main course, would you, Mr. O'Bryan and perhaps offering me a first name?"

Garrett couldn't help the pleasure he felt at her to-the-point delightfulness. "Garrett O'Bryan," he told her, extending a hand across the table.

"Claire Orion." She took the offered hand. "My pleasure."

Her skin was pleasantly soft though her grip was firm. He was impressed. Obviously she was well bred; good blood and great training. His unexpected companion was a stunning package all the way around. He couldn't recall the last time he'd been in the company of one so lovely; if he ever had. This woman was rare on many fronts.

She laughed and Garrett realized he'd held her hand just a little longer than protocol deemed reasonable.

"I was admiring your ring." He tried to cover his embarrassment at being caught up in the sheer enjoyment of the feel of her hand in his as she chuckled and pulled her hand away. It really was a lovely ring. Thank goodness she was wearing it or he didn't know what he'd have said about holding her hand so long.

"It was my mother's -- a gift from her grandmother," Claire offered, gazing lovingly at the ring on the hand he'd just released. "Her wedding set is equally as stunning," she told him, as she thrust her left hand across the table.

Garrett looked at the rings and nodded in agreement. "I'm sorry," he said quietly.

"For?" Her eyes narrowed as she looked at him.

"For the loss of your mother, and at such a young age."

She eyed him suspiciously and grew noticeably tense as she asked, "What makes you think my mother is dead?"

"Sorry. Didn't mean to appear prying. Goes with the profession I suppose."

"And that profession might be...? Her chin was set in a defiant tilt that he didn't understand.

"Psychologist," he told her after a long pause. Her sudden change in demeanor made him hesitant to tell her;

fearful his lovely companion would bolt and he'd find himself finishing the meal alone. "Don't worry," he added as her lips tightened into a thin, straight line. "I don't spend my off hours analyzing those around me, especially when the company is so pleasant."

"Yet you did." She waved her ringed fingers at him.

"Ah, not fair." He pointed at her. "You as much as told me yourself!"

"Really?!" Her voice was riddled with disbelief and distrust. "And I did that by ...?"

"The rings. Your mother might have given you the wedding set had she divorced, though not likely. Most women are peculiar about those things. They either use them to create a different ring or, more times than not, lock them away. Certainly she would be a rare woman who would accept her daughter wearing them and on her left hand at that. Your other ring as well... You said it was a gift to her from her grandmother. Why else would she have parted with them both?" He shrugged, hopeful his explanation would suffice. His eyes pleaded with her to accept it.

She studied him before nodding. Her face relaxed into a mischievous smile and she added, "That would still be analysis and I trust I won't be receiving a bill."

Garrett laughed. "No bill. I promise." He held up two fingers in a scout's promise and Claire smiled, reminding herself she'd better watch what she said from there on.

"So, your date's daughter became ill?" she asked in an attempt to divert the conversation.

Garrett laughed. "Her daughter? Not exactly. Her dog! Though she treats her better than most people treat their children." He rolled his eyes and Claire raised her finely plucked brows in seeming disapproval. "Oh dear. Don't tell me you're one of those people who put their pets above their human friends? You seemed so nearly perfect." He grimaced and Claire laughed heartily.

"Far from perfect and I don't have a dog. I was thinking though…" she stopped, unsure of whether her words could cross boundaries of butting in since she barely knew this man. His love life was none of her business and she knew how people liked to turn the tables when they felt uncomfortable in a conversation. She certainly didn't want to find herself being analyzed again.

Garrett waited for her to continue. "Thinking what?" he prodded when she did not.

She shook her head. "I don't want to be rude."

"I promise I won't take it that way. You've piqued my interest. Don't leave me hanging!" Garrett pretended to pant and beg at the same time.

Claire rolled her eyes. "Well, you don't seem overly thrilled with your girlfriend and her doggie situation. In fact, you don't seem that into her at all." She shrugged.

"Fair assessment. Although she was to be my dinner companion, she's not my girlfriend. We've been out a few times. I wasn't sure it was clicking. Tonight pretty much confirmed it for me." He watched Claire as she put all the pieces together. "Does it all fit?"

She nodded.

"May I ask what you do, Ms. Orion, without you believing yourself under scrutiny?"

Claire watched his brows shoot up, his head tilt in surprise the almost instantaneous look of mischief that covered her face.

"I do as I please, Mr. O'Bryan. Nothing more. Nothing less." She laughed. "You're right. My parents are both dead and I inherited a vast fortune at a young age. Therefore, I've never had to *do* anything."

"And you're okay with that? No dreams you're pursuing? No cause you stamp as your own?" he questioned.

"Ah! That sounds very near analysis to me," she teased with an edge of seriousness.

"Mere conversation" He waved his lifted hands. "You're not exactly dressed for me to request that you lie down on my couch."

Claire could see that he regretted the words as quickly as they'd spewed from his mouth and found the blush that tinted his cheeks rather endearing.

"Fair enough. Couches aren't exactly my first choice for... reclination, relaxation, or recreation, let alone the reading of my mind." He expelled the breath he'd held making her laugh. "Do I scare you... is it actually Mr. or should I be calling you Doctor?"

"First, I've seen enough in these few minutes to realize I should be on guard. I've told myself that a time or two since I sat down, yet I continue to fail to heed my own warnings. And I'm addressed most often as Doctor, though Mr. is perfectly fine with me. I do happen to be that as well, though to my patients and around the office, Doctor seems to be the name I go by."

"Remind me to never ask you a simple question if I'm in a hurry," she laughed.

Garrett couldn't help but react to her sweet melodic laughter. It seemed to come so freely from her, yet there was something guarded about her as well. Was there a hint of sadness, of longing, behind the beautiful, mischievous sparkle of her blue-gray eyes?

"Stop staring. It's disconcerting. I feel as though you're trying to look into my mind." Experience told him she didn't want him in her head, especially tonight of all nights.

He shook his head. "It's just your eyes - they're such an unusual shade of blue. I didn't notice at first. It's almost as if they…"

"They change color… with my moods and feelings or most probably with my blood pressure," she finished his sentence. "Another gift from my dead mother."

She was poking fun at him. At least she could find humor in an undoubtedly trying situation. He wanted to inquire about the particulars of their passing, though he knew she'd accuse him of practicing his profession. He chose a hopefully less sticky subject.

"Ms. Orion, would you mind if we dispensed with the last name formalities? I believe as the champagne loosens my tongue the Orion/O'Bryan similarities may provoke me to an awkward slip. I'll forget which of us is which." They both laughed.

"Garrett, correct?" He nodded. "I'll gladly welcome the switch. Last names are so formally tedious at times; especially when we forget which one belongs to us." Free laughter flowed again.

"Claire it is then." He liked the feel of her name on his tongue. The thought made his brow crinkle. She intoxicated him much more than the champagne. He wondered why.

The meal progressed pleasantly, capped with a shared, decadent, raspberry chocolate dessert.

"Why are we celebrating?" he asked as she dipped her fork into the corner closest to her.

"What would make you say we're celebrating?" She was surprised by his suggestion.

He shrugged, not wanting to ruffle her again in any

way.

Reading his thoughts, she smiled. "You're suddenly wondering, as you did in the beginning, why a woman would get all dressed up and take herself out to a fancy restaurant to dine alone. It seems... dysfunctional? Emotionally unstable? Downright coo coo?"

He looked down at his fork.

"Perhaps I was stood up as well..."

"Nope. You called in for a table," he reminded her.

"Right." She tried to think of something else, though the quantity of champagne they'd consumed made anything short of silly hard to formulate. "We need coffee. I do anyway. Or maybe just a cab. I believe we've practically closed down the place."

Garrett looked around, surprised at the number of empty tables. He looked back at his bewitching dinner partner, remorseful at the thought of this evening coming to an end.

"I have my car. Could I offer you a ride?" he asked, holding his breath in hope.

"It's a big city. How do you know I'm not far out of your way?"

"Statistically people don't venture far from their own zone for a meal." He shrugged. "Am I wrong?"

"Actually I live at the Grange. So your statistic stands, at least for me."

"So? The ride?" He could tell she was debating within herself. After all, she really didn't know him. It was one thing to have dinner with a stranger in a full restaurant. A ride all alone changed the playing field completely. Though as he watched her, secretly analyzing because that's just what he did, Garrett got the distinct feeling his was certainly not the first offer to be taken home she'd received nor accepted.

He smiled as she nodded. "Good," he said. "I wasn't quite ready to part with such a mesmerizing companion."

Claire raised her brows; her eyes dancing playfully as she raked the tip of her teeth over her lower lip.

Garrett's cheeks flamed again and he stammered his response. "I didn't mean to imply... I never expected... I didn't think..."

Claire began to giggle at his uneasy moment.

"Well, I'm glad *you're* finding humor in the moment."

"I apologize," Claire sputtered through her laughter. "Oh, we do clearly travel in different circles, my new-found friend." She dabbed her mirth-filled eyes with a tissue she produced from her bag. "It's been a long time since I've stumbled across anyone with your quality of innocence, Garrett. It's refreshing, actually."

He studied her again. "How old are you, Claire?"

"Is there a qualifying age?" she joked.

He shook his head. "Just curious. You seem to have lived an awful lot for one who I'd say has to be on the lower numeral side of her twenties. You've got a lot going on inside of you."

Their eyes locked. Claire was quiet. Had it not been for the champagne she might have bolted. She didn't want him to see inside of her.

Her moment of seriousness was replaced by that ever-present, barely masked mischievousness. "Experience is a great teacher. You should know that, Mr. Analyst. And a ride home *only* will suffice, if the offer is still on the table."

"It is and I'll go ahead and thank you for the continued honor of your company," he said and they both laughed. Claire looked at him in that knight in shining armor awe that always made him cringe. He knew from experience that he was no savior. As hard as he'd tried, he'd failed miserably in that department. But that wasn't something he was going to dwell on. Not tonight anyway. Not with Claire Orion sitting across from him.

# Chapter 3

Garrett didn't see it, though Claire must have indicated that they were ready to leave. Anthony appeared and leaned toward her, whispering that there would be no check.

"Your meal is on the house due to the mistake," he told her quietly.

"As expected," she answered, discreetly handing him a couple of large bills. "There will be no need for change."

The waiter stared at her for a moment before realization set in and a look of gratitude and delight covered his features. "Thank you." He half bowed as he went away. Claire glanced at Garrett who watched her with a look of awe. A class act with an unmistakable edge of sheer rawness all rolled up into one perfect bundle.

"Shall we?" she asked when she was finished with whatever it was she was doing beneath the edge of the table.

Garrett nodded. "You know," he said as he scooted her chair back, "you really should let me take care of our dear Mr. Ballard. I didn't realize you'd already made arrangements with the waiter. I'd have protested but you seem the type not to take interference lightly."

"You're right," she teased. "Never undermine or second guess me and all will go well between us," she continued in a silly English accent, "and I shan't hear anymore of your nonsense. Now come along and watch the pro in action." She crooked her finger and winked as she walked away. Garrett followed, unsure if he was bemused or bewitched. He felt fairly certain about one thing, Mr. Ballard was about to find himself asking the same question.

Secured within Garrett's jet black Lexus, Claire and Garrett both burst into laughter.

"Oh, that was priceless." Garrett was able to speak only as his laughter subsided somewhat. "That poor man... Oh, Claire, you really had him certain his job was on the block. And such a pleasant look upon your angelic face as you delivered the blow."

"Oh, I'm truly evil in heels, aren't I?" She looked apologetic for a full split second before breaking into more laughter. "He was happy when I kissed his cheek and pulled my hand free of his." She waved her hand back and forth.

"Yes, once he realized you were putting him on."

Claire shrugged. "Evil!"

Garrett shook his head. "Playful and, perhaps, a bit ornery. Evil? I don't think so." He smiled at her as Claire studied his face. Uncertainty clouded her beautiful features. She looked away, staring out her window as they drove a couple of blocks in silence.

"How long have you lived at the Grange?" he asked. "I heard they're very hard units to get hold of."

Claire's nod confirmed that they were. "We've had the unit forever," she told him then laughed. "Well, Dad had it. Acquired it many years ago, along with his first mistress."

Garrett's mouth fell open. Claire nodded again and laughed. "You're surprised that I know, am so nonchalant about it, that she was his first, or that we'd keep the unit?"

"Yes... all of the above."

"Boy! For all the stories you're sure to hear in your line of work, you sure are naïve," she poked. He started to protest then decided she was right.

"The woman faded away, my mom liked the unit, and it became our place to stay when we came to town. He loved my mom, Garrett. The other women were mere diversions. My mom was the only true wife he had."

Garrett couldn't believe what he was hearing. Had he known her better he'd have told her that was crap. He'd have asked her what about vows and respect? "Well, it's a beautiful building, at least from the outside. I've never been in," he said instead.

"You want to come up? We can have that coffee we never ordered..." They were stopped in front of the building waiting for a clearing to turn into the circle drive where the doorman waited. Their eyes locked and a bucket of emotions passed between them.

He reached over and touched her cheek. "I want to, but I won't. Besides, I have a brunch date at my parent's farm in Morgan's Falls. It's late and I'll have to get up early to make it on time."

"Oh." Claire nodded, the corners of her lips turning down. "A decent reason I suppose." She chuckled. "I've never been turned down for parents."

They smiled at one another as he pulled in and the doorman approached. "Another time perhaps?"

Claire gave a noncommittal half shrug. "Perhaps." She was silent for a moment, signaling the doorman to wait. "Thank you for an enjoyable evening, Garrett. I'm pleased our paths crossed." When she reached for the door, he grabbed her arm, stopping her motion. She looked at his hand then at him.

"I have this overwhelming feeling that I'll never see you again once you get out." His brows were drawn down, concern and disappointment shadowing his face.

The sound of Claire's heartbeat whooshed in her ears. She sucked in a breath and stared at him. Could he hear the loud thudding of her heart?

"Let me have your phone." She expelled the breath

she'd been holding and held out her hand expecting him to produce his phone, which he did without question. She studied it for a moment then keyed in her number. "There." She handed it back.

"Thank you." He smiled, rubbing the phone between his fingers as if it was her hand. "We'll have that coffee… and sooner than you think.

"Would we have had coffee, Dr. O'Bryan?" she asked, kissing his cheek and bolting from the car before he had time to recover.

When she waved and smiled mischievously from the lobby doorway he shook his head and laughed. The thought of her would not easily be shaken, he was sure of that.

"You're home early, Ms. Orion," Garrett heard the doorman saying to her as he pushed the button that rolled down the window. "And alone! You ruffled somebody's feathers again, girl?"

Claire started to respond but was cut off by Garrett's voice calling her name. She turned toward him and he was struck momentarily silent by her beauty. Uncertain of his intent, she walked back to the car and looked through the open window.

"Change your mind?" she teased. "No, I suppose Morgan's Falls still has you bound. What then?"

"Sunday brunch? 10:00ish? And we'll have that coffee then. Scouts honor." He held up two fingers.

"Wouldn't you know. Friday night and I get stuck with a parent whipped boy scout." She laughed, letting him know she was still teasing. "Make it 10:30 and I'll accept with expectation."

Garrett nodded. "Claire," he called as she began to back away. "You seem as though you'd be a woman of your word" When she didn't respond he added, "I'm right about that, am I not?"

Claire breathed in and held it for a moment as she looked into the distance. The night had not gone as she'd planned. Now he was questioning her. Why would he ask her that? If she said yes, under the circumstances, was she bound by her word? Exhaling, she nodded. "My yes is yes. I'll be waiting and watching. 10:30 sharp on Sunday morning."

Garrett smiled. "Thank you."

"You may change your mind. You don't really know me." She raised a brow and pushed away from his car.

He shook his head. No, he didn't know her, but he did believe their paths had crossed that evening for a definite reason. Too many things had fallen into place to make it happen for it to have been coincidental. He wondered if he'd ever find out why.

"You losin' your touch, Miss?" Garrett heard the doorman teasing her again.

"Nah, Charlie. I got lucky in a different way tonight." She elbowed the older gentleman. "I found me an angel. What was his name? Clarence maybe? Oh listen... I think I hear a bell ringing."

He heard the doorman chuckle as Claire disappeared behind the heavy wood and beveled glass doors of the grand building.

"Not an angel with these thoughts!" he whispered as he drove away.

# Chapter 4

Claire sat down on the edge of her bed to remove her shoes. She laid her phone on the nightstand next to the two waiting pill bottles then pulled off her earrings and placed them next to the phone. Her fingers trembling, she picked up the pill bottles and placed her empty hand over her heart. For the first time in a very long time she hadn't thought about the hurt inside for several hours. Maybe Garrett really was an angel. He'd certainly altered the course of her life, she thought, opening the nightstand drawer and dropping the bottles inside.

Garrett was right. It was late and she was suddenly very, very tired. With a clipped half-laugh, she looked at her phone and shook her head. She hadn't even gotten his number. Now the true question… was *he* a man of *his* word? Would he show on Sunday morning?

As she stood up to head into the connecting bathroom, her phone began to play its jingle. "Hello?" she spoke into it.

"Funny thing... as I was driving home, I realized two things," The sound of Garrett's voice met her ear through the phone.

"And those two things would be what, Dr. O'Bryan?"

Claire could imagine his lips curving upward and she couldn't help but smile. "You left your scarf/wrap thingy in my car. It smells wonderful, by the way. And you have no way to get hold of me should you need to."

Claire's laughter echoed around her room, the sincerity of it feeling so much better than she could have imagined. "I thought you were an angel, Dr. O'Bryan, but I think you're a mind reader instead."

"Perhaps," he answered. "Most likely I was thinking how nice it would be to hear your voice and what an ego booster it would be if you called, when I realized you didn't have my number."

"Well, now I do, and I thank you for thinking of calling. But I do have to ask… how do you know my wrap smells good?"

Garrett laughed. "I knew you'd catch me on that one the moment the words left my mouth. You never disappoint, do you Claire?"

"I certainly try not to…"

The conversation continued with the expected tones and easy, volleying banter for a few minutes. Each stated again how much they had enjoyed meeting the other and that they were looking forward to their brunch.

"Goodnight, Garrett," Claire's voice, light but tired, spoke the words that would close their evening.

"Yes, it was a good night, wasn't it?" he asked. "See you Sunday."

# Chapter 5

Claire was surprised to see it was nearing 10:00 the next morning when her eyes finally fluttered open to stay. After a moment's hesitation she threw back the covers and climbed from the comfort of the silky sheets. The carpet was soft beneath her bare feet. Her robe caressed her body with a velvety delight and Claire realized her senses were on edge. She was feeling life full out. No drugs, scant alcohol, no man to share her bed. This was reality.

Another reality hit her as she entered the bathroom and met her own reflection in the etched mirror. The deeply cut lines in the glass framed her like a beautiful portrait. As she stared at herself, she realized how easily she may not have awakened that morning. Had it not been for the chance crossing of paths with Garrett… he really was her Clarence.

"I am not worthless," she whispered to no one. "No matter what he said…" Trying to ignore the doubt that reflected from her eyes, she closed them as the tears welled. "I can be something to someone…" A sob replaced her words as the tears began to fall. She didn't bother to stop them. It had been a very long time since she'd cried.

Throughout her long, steamy shower the tears flowed. Claire felt refreshed, purged when she emerged from the glass cage and had the overwhelming desire to do something she hadn't done in years… paint. With a smile she toweled off, dressed quickly and headed to the sunroom.

Claire opened the double doors that led into the spacious corner room. The light filled her eyes, flooding in from the floor to ceiling windows on two sides meeting in the far corner. Claire had always loved this room. It had been her favorite place as a child; a haven and a place where fond memories were made. This was the one room Claire had left untouched after her parent's death when she'd moved into the unit full-time. The sunroom needed no redecorating to reflect her. It had always been *her* room.

She pulled open the carved wooden doors of the spacious storage closet and marveled at its contents just as she had as a little girl. She looked over the vast array of art supplies, so well stocked it rivaled the local craft shop. She wondered how many of her supplies had gone bad after years of non-use.

With a deep breath she picked up the old market basket and began to fill it with whatever she believed she'd need. Brushes, jar, pallet, paint tubes... She tucked a canvas board under her arm and grabbed a folded tabletop easel. Satisfied, she pushed the doors closed with her foot and went to the table by the windows.

What a view, she thought as she looked out over the city with a renewed love for the sights. She wondered if Garrett had met his destination and was now in the throws of a country brunch. She smiled as she turned back to setting up her table.

Two hours later, Claire was satisfied with her creation. It was different and perhaps not as good as some of her past work. After all, it had been years since she'd painted; not since her father had said it was a worthless pursuit and would take her nowhere. The cancer had hit right after that; another blow to her usefulness in life, according to dear old Daddy.

Claire fought against the pain. Her whole life she'd tried to please him. And then she'd tried to show him he was right. That had almost resulted in her own end. She looked at the painting; an angel slightly resembling Garrett reaching out to an unseen victim. Only her hands were visible. They were Claire's hands, wearing her mother's rings. The fingertips of the left hands were barely touching.

Claire was suddenly starving as well as being struck with an overwhelming desire to see an old friend. She quickly rinsed her brushes, returned her supplies to the closet, and busied herself with the task of looking presentable.

Old Joe… she thought about her friend. She wondered if he'd remember her. Five years was a long time.

A quick bite eaten at the corner deli as she watched the crowd bustling by reminded her there was hardly ever not a crowd in the historic neighborhood. She looked across the way to her building and counted up the rows of glass windows to where she'd sat not long before. She was glad to belong to the history; to be a *living* part.

With intentioned slowness, Claire strolled the three blocks to Old Joe's art gallery. She knew it was still there. She'd seen it, even seen him a time or two from behind the windows of a cab or looking out of a would-be suitor's car.

The chimes jingled as she opened the creaky old door, pressing hard as the sign directed.

"Be with you in a couple," the familiar voice called from somewhere in back. "Feel free to look around."

"Take your time. I'm in no hurry," Claire hollered back. Joe immediately came through the drape covered doorway.

"Little Claire Orion. I thought you'd left me for good, Angel." He came toward her and she hugged him tightly, blinking back unwanted tears.

"Just took a wrong turn, Joe. Thanks for welcoming me

back on course with open arms." She patted his scruffy cheek as he released her. "It looks like you're doing well, old friend." She gestured to all the pieces of artwork and the vast number with sold tags.

Joe smiled and nodded. "Thanks to you." He chuckled. "From a street vendor being told to pack up or else, to a shop owner. All because a perfect little girl made some mighty big demands on her wealthy father."

"Even that little girl was far from perfect, Joe. We both know that. Besides, this old shop was just sitting idle because it wasn't pretty enough for one of his own ventures. To be honest, he paid me off because I knew who the woman was who had vacated it." She elbowed Old Joe. "It didn't take a rocket scientist to know his only interest in an artist would be the pictures she could paint in his bed."

"Now, now Missy. No speaking ill of the dead." They both laughed, though Joe's face sobered quickly. "I worried about you after I heard about their accident. Tried to get in touch with you but they shooed me away up there at your big fancy building. Think they thought Old Joe was a gold digger when all I wanted was to check on my angel. No Ma'am - always wanted to make my way doing exactly what I love. And thanks to you, I been doing just that for nearly thirteen years now." He hugged her again.

"I'm sorry I never came back, Joe."

"Ah. You're here now. Let it go. Always look forward, Angel. No matter what you've been through or what life throws at you, the future has the potential to hold greatness. Don't you ever forget that." He led her to a small table in the back. "I don't suppose you want milk and cookies anymore. Look at you. What a fine woman you made. Though there was no doubt in that coming about."

Claire laughed. She felt like the same little girl inside,

especially here with Joe. "How about tea?" she asked him. "You always had tea when I had my milk."

Joe nodded and began preparing their drinks. "You still paint, Claire? I still have requests for your work. I kept the last three, marked sold but still on display. People always want them."

"I painted this morning for the first time in five years, Joe. It wasn't a great piece, but it's a beginning at least."

Joe nodded, glancing back over his shoulder at Claire. She looked away.

"When they took away my ability to make babies, I thought I could still leave a legacy with my artwork, you know. Then *he* told me it was all worthless, all of it. He made me feel completely insignificant and I wanted to die. Only he died instead and I threw myself into becoming numb. Until last night." She looked back at her old friend as he sat down their glasses and slid into the chair opposite hers. She'd always talked openly with Joe. He'd listened without judgment for all those years while she harbored the pain of her father's rejection. He'd tried to be a positive male role model in her life. But a father's love and approval, or lack thereof, was hard, if not impossible to replace.

"And last night?" Joe prodded, his tone as gentle as ever.

Claire smiled. "I'd planned to end it all. Instead I went out for a final meal and met my own angel. I don't know how it will all end, Joe. I don't even know him. All I know is that I didn't do what I'd planned, and I got up this morning and painted, then came to see you." They stared at each other then laughed. Old Joe reached for her hand and gently squeezed it.

"I'm so glad you did."

"Me too." She nodded. "Me too."

They talked for over two hours with little interruption before a group came in that Joe knew would require his full attention.

"You know, Claire, I've got a couple of kids I'd like you to meet. They come by every now and again... live just down the street. They remind me of another little girl I used to know." He gently elbowed her side while she helped him clear their dishes.

Claire quietly rinsed the glasses, contemplating where Joe was going with his comment.

"There are a lot of people who seem to have it all. But, inside they're eaten up with self-doubt and hurt. Sometimes all they need is someone to help them learn to believe in themselves. You rich kids... nobody ever seems to think you have a care in the world. And, even if they did know, they have no idea how to help."

"What are you saying, Joe? How could I help? I couldn't even help myself." Her face looked pinched, uncertain.

Joe shrugged. "Look inside, Angel. What could have helped you make that turn before last night?"

Claire seemed distant. She was wondering whether it would have made a difference if someone within her own ranks had told her that her dreams mattered, that what she wanted to pursue was all right. She'd had Joe. But her dad didn't respect him. Would it have mattered?

"Think on it," Joe whispered as he steered her toward the front of the shop and changed the subject. "Can I expect more paintings then? I'd like to take the sold sign off those three up there. The gentleman in the dark blue has been after them for a while now."

Claire looked at the paintings from a distance. She hesitated. "I'll try to paint you some more, though I'm afraid I may have lost my touch along with my heart. What say we let him have two? Keep the one with the little girl. I'd forgotten all about her, but for some reason, I don't want to let her go."

"Artist's whimsy," Joe chuckled and motioned for her to go before him. The group eyed them as he hugged her at the front door. "When do you see him again?" he whispered.

"Who?" Claire asked. She was watching the group admiring her painting, though the gentleman in blue was openly admiring her. She smiled at him which, of course, he returned.

"Flirt!" Joe teased. "Shall I introduce you? No, no. You're to meet your angel. When?"

"What makes you think I'm meeting him again?" she asked, the surprise causing her to step back.

'It's Old Joe, Claire."

She hugged him tightly. "10:30 tomorrow. Sunday brunch."

"Come see me soon, Angel."

Claire nodded and left. She saw Old Joe removing the sold tag from her paintings and knew he must have told the group she was the artist because they all turned to stare at her through the window. She kept walking. She'd return in a few days to give Old Joe her phone number and he'd surprise her with a request for new pieces.

She wondered if Old Joe remembered their deal -- half to him and half to the childrens' center. He'd remember. He was Old Joe.

# Chapter 6

Sunday morning found Claire unusually nervous as she watched the clock, waiting for the minute hand to tell her it was time to go down to the lobby. She'd actually done a little more painting after she'd left Old Joe the day before and had found her artwork had changed. It lacked the lightness of her younger work, yet it held a depth she hadn't noticed before. She thought of the painting of the little girl she'd told Old Joe to hold. It held qualities of both. Claire smiled to herself, smoothing a hand over her no longer dark hair as she remembered what she'd told Old Joe when she took the picture to him.

"That's my little girl, Joe," she'd said.

"You with a blondie with all those dark curls of yours? Hmm. I don't see it, Angel."

"You've always called me that, Joe, though I'm not sure why. Everyone knows angels are only in Heaven. Besides, I can't be one. Just ask my dad. He says I've got the devil in me and, like all women, I'm already learning to use it to get my own way." Her scrunched face a pretty good indication that she was hurt and confused by her father's statement.

"Ah little lady, you're both right and wrong." He'd shaken his head. "But the devil... I don't see that at all. Seems to me you're just acting like the adults around you."

She nodded, her young mind trying to process what he'd said. "How is that right and wrong?"

"Well," he began, sliding a plate of cookies and glass of milk in front of her. He sat down across from his beautiful angel. "True angels are in heaven. But they're also all around us."

"Really?" Her wide eyes held both concern and uncertainty.

"Really." He nodded. "I'm pretty sure you've got one standing beside you right now."

Claire's eyes got big as she turned to look and, of course, saw nothing. Still she'd shuddered a bit and kept glancing to her side.

Joe had chuckled as he continued. "Then there are those certain people that will cross your path along your walk of life. They'll change your course for the good or bad. Those who change it for the better - you have to wonder if they weren't sent by God. Those are the people I call angels. Perhaps an earthly angel of sorts… that's what you are to me, Claire." He reached across and touched her cheek. She smiled and kissed his paint splattered old hand.

"I think you're one too, Joe. For me at least."

"Nah." He'd looked at her with such intense wisdom she couldn't help but believe his words that followed. "You'll have your angels, Claire. Old Joe isn't one of them. But they'll come. You watch. You'll see."

"I think you're wrong… about you, I mean. But I'll watch for the others too." She'd smiled the smile of a contented child and went back to devouring her cookies. Joe had smiled his own smile as he'd leaned back and took a long sip of his tea.

And there it was, years later, her without the ability to have children and him still holding the painting… the painting of her little girl. Claire's face dropped, disappointment washing over her. Maybe the reason she couldn't let it go was because the girl in the painting was the only little girl she'd ever have.

She glanced over the other works she'd painted the day before, fixating momentarily on the one of Garrett as the angel.

Joe had always called her his angel because she'd helped him get set up in his business location and even talked her dad into signing over the deed to him and paying the bills until the old artist was able to stand on his own two feet. Claire wondered if everyone in life had someone who'd been sent to save them.

She grabbed her wrap and headed down to wait for Garrett. "Please be real," she whispered into the empty elevator. As the doors opened, she was greeted with his smiling face. She glanced at her watch.

"You're not late," he told her. His grin widened as she caressed his offered arm when she slipped her hand through the crook.

"I thought maybe we could stroll up the street to Hannigans?"

"Stroll?" She hitched an eyebrow and they laughed. "Good choice, actually." She smiled up at him and lightly pinched his arm.

"What's that for?"

She shrugged. "Just checking to make sure you're real." They both laughed again as they stepped out into the late morning air. "I'd half expected that I'd dreamed you up and you'd be a no-show this morning."

"I think I'm the one who's dreaming," he told her.

"Ah! Flattery. Keep talking," she teased.

They continued with the playful flirtations as they walked; each content with the reality that held them.

"So, how was country brunch with Mum?" she asked when they were seated and the waiter had moved on, leaving them to look over their menus.

"Mum… and the rest of the family. It was delicious. Can't beat homemade country cooking. You'll have to join me sometime."

Claire nearly choked on her response. "That's a bit presumptuous for two people who have just met, don't you think?"

Garrett shrugged.

"Let me guess. You already told your mom about me?"

"Guilty." Garrett winced. "Am I that transparent? Is that a bad thing? That I told her I mean?"

"Again presumptuous, but flattering. I have that effect on people," she teased.

He smiled at her as the waiter returned. It was a smile that told her she'd had an effect on him, all kidding aside.

Claire liked the way he was looking at her. She liked that he'd told his mom about her and even the fact that he'd consider taking her home.

"Did you grow up in Morgan's Falls?" she asked while they waited.

"No. We had a place just off of Shay and McCarthy." Claire nodded indicating she knew where it was. "I'm not too far from there now. There's a school nearby and they have that great park…"

"I know the one. It's been there forever. My mom and I used to go back when swings and merry-go-rounds weren't lawsuits waiting to happen. So, your parents… they just up and moved? How long ago?"

Garrett shifted in his seat, looking away before answering. "A couple of years."

Claire could have sworn he was wrestling with whether he should say more than what he did. When he finally answered, she nodded and looked down, pretending to flick something off the table. Her question had noticeably altered the mood and she was glad when the waiter returned to take their order . The conversation would undoubtedly take a different course when it resumed.

As the waiter left their table, Claire's attention was caught by a small child two tables down. Garrett watched her watching the little girl's animated antics. She turned back to him with an amused smile.

"They seem to have their hands full." She laughed.

"That's a two year old for you," Garrett agreed. "So I suppose you see yourself with a whole passel of kids?"

She shook her head and looked back at the little girl still giving her parents a run for their money. "I wouldn't have minded one or two..." Her voice was noticeably softer. She sighed then looked back and shrugged.

He studied her for a minute, then casually said, "So, Claire, tell me more about yourself."

The you've-got-to-be-kidding look on Claire's face caused Garrett to burst into laughter that garnered looks from the occupants of the tables nearby. "Too psychologistish huh?" he said more quietly.

"Quite!" she teased. "You do have a way of pulling out that couch, don't you?"

He nodded and shrugged his apology.

"What could I tell you? I'm quite shallow actually." He began to protest, which she ignored and went on. "You already know I'm a poor, orphaned, rich girl and that I don't do much of anything... Oh! I know something you'll never guess. I paint."

"Really? Paint as in ..." he coaxed. She knew what he was doing and decided to toy with him.

"Walls and stuff," she shrugged. "Houses, buildings, a little subway graffiti every now and again."

Claire could tell by the drawn brows and the way he worked his jaw that he was trying hard to determine whether he should believe her or not. She maintained her serious delivery for a few more seconds before a smile broke through.

"Oh what a priceless expression. Almost as good as the look on Mr. Ballard's face when he thought his job was on the line," she laughed then reached over, without thought, to pat his hand. He jumped at her unexpected touch. They stared at each other, then he surprised her by grasping her hand and bringing her fingers to his lips.

"The hand of an artist. I hope you'll show me your work sometime. And I really need to remember what I kept forgetting the other night."

"And what was that?" she asked enjoying the continued warmth of his gaze.

"That I must always be on guard around you!" He kissed her hand again then released it.

The warm feeling remained as she clasped her hands together beneath the table and the date continued, lapsing into casual comfort.

It was nearing 1:00 when they left the restaurant and headed back toward her building, their pace a slow, casual stroll. Neither of them were in a hurry to have their time together end.

"Ah! You found a spot to park. Amazing. They're not always easy to come by," Claire commented as they paused beside his car a few spaces down from the circle drive that marked the entrance to her building. "You can always tell the doorman you're here to visit me and they'll give you a pass for the garage."

Garrett smiled sheepishly. "So, does that statement serve as permission to call on you again?" he asked.

"Hmm. I suppose it does, as well as alleviating the awkward situation of you trying to figure out how to ask me."

He shook his head. "You really are borderline wicked."

She nodded in agreement and they both laughed.

"So? Are we making another date or is it just an open invite; the old I'll call you sometime approach?" she asked.

"You know, Claire, you should really try being less bashful. Don't be afraid to speak your mind," he teased.

"Oh, Doctor. If I truly did speak my mind even your psychologist training wouldn't keep you from being shocked." Claire smiled her most wicked smile as she leaned toward him.

Garrett swallowed hard. She ran her hand down his arm and he shuddered.

"Women in your circles aren't so forward?" She tried to sound demure. "Perhaps they just don't know how to ask for what they want." She reached up and kissed him.

"Claire." Her name was only a breath on his lips. He gazed down at her through heavy lids. "As much as I'd love to pursue your train of thought..."

"I know. It's that darn boy scout blood of yours." She looked away to hide the feeling of rejection. Men never told her no.

"I don't want to sound preachy but doesn't what you're suggesting entail even a smidgen of commitment?" he blurted out.

"Why? It takes a lot less of the getting-to-know-you conversation than the dates we've had," she told him.

"But... intimacy! It's so..." he fought for a word.

"Intimate!" she added sarcastically. She rolled her eyes. "Come on, Garrett. Tell me you're not just a little bit interested." She pressed against him, molding herself to him, surprised he didn't immediately step away.

"I never said I wasn't interested, Claire. I just prefer getting to know a woman. Starting here." He pointed to her head. "And here." He pulled back and traced a heart across her skin, just above the neckline of her low-cut shirt. "Then…" He brushed her nose with his own before letting his lips meet hers. She felt his arms tighten around her as he deepened the kiss, his tongue darting out, tentatively at first, and then demanding her lips to part, which they did. It was a simple kiss on a busy sidewalk that still left her breathless.

When he pulled away, she stared up at him for a moment, fighting for air in shallow gasps. "You confuse me," she said as she pushed away from him.

"Seems pretty straight forward to me," he laughed. "And, how about lunch Wednesday? Can you meet me at Louie's at 1:00? I have the afternoon free."

"Free for?" she asked with the same sarcastic tone.

"Free for not having to rush away if we end up having another two and a half hour meal. If our history holds true, we seem to need a couple of hours minimum."

She smiled. "Are you sure you're not an angel in a handsome man's clothing?" she asked as she kissed him again, a light peck on the cheek.

The desire in his gaze gave her the answer. Another smile and she walked away.

"See you on Wednesday," she called over her shoulder knowing he'd remain where he was, watching her go, until she'd disappeared behind the heavy doors of her building. A quick glance back as Charlie opened the doors told her she was right.

# Chapter 7

Just inside the door of Louie's Pub and Grille, Garrett waited, pleasure evident on his face as Claire crossed the threshold.

"Do you ever not look like a million bucks?" he asked as he kissed her cheek.

"Only when I look like a trillion," she teased. As always happened, heads turned as they were escorted to their table.

"I presume you can't tell me about your day, so I won't even ask. How about whatever it is you do to fill your hours when you're not at your office?" she asked as they waited for their salads.

"Well, I spend a lot of time reading and going over cases..."

"No. I mean in your off time. When you're not working," she interrupted as she squeezed lemon over her freshly delivered salad.

"No dressing?" He scrunched his face, ignoring her question.

"Not as healthy," she told him, "but feel free. I won't lecture if you slather your rabbit food in mouth watering goodness. Gee. It does sound better that way. Okay, you've convinced me." She reached for the bottle of dressing and poured it on. "What?"

He was shaking his head. "You know people who manage to be easily persuaded or talk themselves into things are good candidates for my services," he teased.

"Very funny. I'm trying to be more receptive to new and different. I took a chance in meeting you again, didn't I?" she teased. "And you never answered my question."

"That is what I do. What? It can be enjoyable," he protested when she rolled her eyes. "What should I be doing? Frequenting clubs and seducing beautiful women – a different one for every night of the week? Not sure that would be good for my practice."

"Point given," she conceded. "So you just read all your notes…"

"Not exactly. I look over them or think about sessions. I try to come at them from all different angles. I have to admit it's quite a rush seeing the light of change or realization come across someone. That's when I know I've truly helped them and they can continue on with normal life."

"What is normal, Garrett? Isn't that a hegemonic reality? One man's normal may be total chaos and lunacy to another."

"You're right, of course, and that's partly why I look for alternate ways of helping people find the bridge. I enjoy it."

"So I suppose you always wanted to be a psychologist?" she asked.

"Actually, I wasn't quite sure what I wanted to be. I knew I liked helping people and getting inside to see if I could figure out what made them tick. My parents were great about helping me explore alternatives and understanding where my passions lay then grasping hold of those passions to fulfillment."

Claire couldn't help but feel his excitement. She also felt a twinge of envy that he had been so nurtured by his parents. She wondered what it would have been like had her dad embraced her love of art and helped her pursue it. Her mom, of course, loved everything she did and helped as much as she could - so long as it didn't ruffle Daddy's feathers.

"Of course, I also wanted to be a gymnast," he told her.

"You're joking!" She eyed him. Surely he couldn't be serious. "Garrett, I think you lie as well as I do!"

He laughed. "Actually, I did take gymnastics as a young

boy and loved it, but… well… my height kind of got in the way as I aged. I enjoyed horseback riding too. That old stables on the far side of the river front. Dad and I used to go there nearly every Saturday. He always loved horses."

"Is that why they moved to the country?"

Garrett shook his head no. "That was his dream, but…"

"Dr. O'Bryan!" The excited female voice cut him off.

"Victoria. How nice to see you. You look well. How are things going?" Standing, Garrett clasped hands with the young woman around Claire's age. She leaned in forcing him to kiss her cheek to avoid an obvious snub.

Claire rolled her eyes. Garrett shrugged, though slight enough that only Claire detected it.

"I'm splendid, Dr. Dreadfully splendid. You know how it is for me." She made a roller coaster wave motion with her hand indicating life's ups and downs. "I probably shouldn't have stopped seeing you," she said in a more quiet, conspiratorial tone. She put her hand to her mouth as though she had an intimate secret then glanced for the first time at Claire.

"Hello, Tori." Claire's voice was cool.

After a momentary loss of composure the other woman regained herself. "Claire. Darling. What a surprise. I had no idea you knew Dr. O'Bryan."

"A mutual shock." Claire glanced at Garrett who was assessing the situation with an air of surprise himself. She bit her lip to keep from laughing, enjoying Garrett's transparency. She could practically see the thoughts inside his head, imagined him wondering whether he should step in to diffuse any biting and clawing that might accompany the hissing and raised backs. He waited.

"So, I never realized you did lunch appointments, Doctor. Is that something new? What a novel idea. Perhaps I'll have to make an appointment…"

Claire cut her off. "Actually, Tori. Darling. I'm not a patient. I'm a *date*."

Garrett closed his eyes as the words were spoken by his beautiful companion, opening them to see a slack-jawed Tori looking back and forth between him and Claire. Claire smiled ever so very sweetly, then continued eating her salad.

"You… are… a… a work of art, Claire Orion. You just have your finger in everybody's pie," Tori fumed. "And you!" She turned to Garrett, tapping his chest with a finely manicured pointer finger. "I'd have thought you smart enough to know better than to get mixed up with the likes of *her*." She turned, nearly tripping in her too-high heels and marched from the restaurant.

Garrett stared after his patient. Ex-patient. Slowly shaking his head and blinking a few times, he collapsed back into his chair and turned to look at Claire.

"What?" She scrunched her shoulders and continued to eat her salad.

"You do realize you managed to undo months of therapy in a matter of minutes, don't you?" He asked her.

"Oh fooey! Tori Johansen doesn't need therapy. She's nothing' but a spoiled, rotten bit… bih, ba, be, buh, buh bazillionaire heiress," she fished for a replacement word to the one she really wanted to use at his look of reproach. "What she really needs is to be turned over someone's knee and delivered a good, hard swat!" Her fork clanked against her place as she dropped it and pushed back slightly from the table to cross her arms over her chest.

Garrett shook his head, trying hard not to laugh. "Opinions aren't allowed in the world of psychology, you know." He smiled and she softened up a bit. "I do have to ask because I'm dying of curiosity. You were the other woman in the boyfriend incident, weren't you?"

"You're not supposed to discuss cases. Patient-doctor privilege or something," she dodged.

"You were!"

Claire rolled her eyes. "I did her a favor with that one. He was no good." She glanced away and continued under her breath, "in more ways than one."

Garrett laughed. "You really are a work of art," he told her.

"I like art, don't you?" she teased as their meal continued with a light air.

"You like movies?" Claire asked as they talked. "You mentioned the old stables at the park. What about the refurbished theater? They just happen to have a Wednesday afternoon matinee…" she fished.

"I forgot all about that old place. What do they show?" He seemed genuinely interested.

Claire smiled. She'd allowed him another easy bridging of events. That was one of her gifts… she had a way with people, with making them feel at ease and instinctively knowing what they needed and how to help them get it. With most people, anyway. Certainly she hadn't had that with her father. She pushed away thoughts of him along with a momentary frown, pleased to find they shared an interest in older movies and that two of the Grand Lady's screens were reserved for exactly that.

"… but you're not really dressed for a stroll around the park and a trip to the theater," he commented on what seemed the obvious.

"Oh, come on! Here, watch this…" She pulled the clips

from her hair and fluffed it about her face and shoulders. She readjusted the neckline of her shirt as he watched with gaping mouth, then stood to reposition her belt and pull her leggings to expose more flesh. "Now all I need is a piece of gum and everyone will think I'm one of the park hookers."

"You really have no restraint, do you?" He stood and reached for his wallet. "And we need to get out of here because everyone is staring." He took her arm and they began to walk toward the cashier.

Claire laughed then whispered, "You do know what people do with hookers, don't you? We could bypass the movies all together."

He shook his head. "You look perfect for the park, Claire. Absolutely perfect."

"Put your wallet away then before people think you're getting ready to pay me."

"But… the meal…"

"Already taken care of," she continued in whispered tones.

"Thank you, Ms. Orion," the cashier called as she steered Garrett toward the door.

Leaving the restaurant, they decided to grab Garrett's car just in case. It turned out to be a good thing. The movie schedule had changed, giving them all of fifteen minutes to spare.

"Garrett?" Claire whispered after they'd settled into their seats.

"Hmm?" He leaned closer to hear her.

"How much time did you spend mulling over Tori's file?" she asked.

Garrett couldn't suppress a soft chuckle. "None. In fact, I quickly came to the same conclusion you did."

"What was that?" she giggled, knowing but wanting to hear him say it anyway.

"That she was a spoiled little rich girl that needed a good old fashioned spanking. Not too unlike another young lady I know that needs to quit paying for everything. It's getting a bit embarrassing." He raised his brows as he looked down his nose at her.

"Oh! The Dr. doesn't like being a kept man?" she teased.

"Careful now. Kept implies commitment which we both know you're highly allergic to."

She laughed again and wound her arm through his as the lights dimmed. She laid her head against his shoulder with the beginning of the movie and he kissed the top of her curls. She'd left it free even though she'd repositioned the rest of her wardrobe. Park prostitute. Garrett thought not. Claire Orion was lady through and through, no matter whatever else she tried to be.

Thus began their Sunday brunches and Wednesday lunches with an occasional matinee and usually at least one dinner a week thrown in. It was an easy, enjoyable relationship that seemed to include an unspoken promise from them both to take things slow in every way.

A good three months flew by before he approached the subject of her making the Saturday trip with him to his parents. He was met with immediate rejection and let it die quickly. They may be taking it slow, but it hadn't stopped his brain from thinking about a possible future any more than it had his body reminding him what a desirable, beautiful woman she was. Still, he knew her feelings well enough not to push it. For some reason, she openly admitted that she was unfit to play the part of a proper wife. Garrett felt sure he could change her view, in time. Until then, he'd proceed carefully and simply enjoy being with her.

# Chapter 8

"I'm not seeing anyone else, Garrett," she told him one day, rather out of the blue.

"Me either, unless you count all those patients who file in and out of my office," he teased, though she could tell he was glad she'd chosen to share that bit of information with him, even if she really couldn't understand it. Commitment still remained an allusive part of her vocabulary... at least, she thought it did. She wondered what made Garrett stick around, considering he really seemed more the settling down type. Then again, his weekly trips to the country... he obviously hadn't managed to untie the strings of childhood. Maybe the relationship fit him as well as it did her. There was only one thing lacking as far as Claire was concerned. She missed the physical, craved the chance to get close to Garrett. She smiled, confident that too would change in time.

"Will you come up?" she whispered as he kissed her lips, cheek, neck. Her eyes fluttered closed and then opened again. He could see a hint of confidence in her gaze, a knowing that he wanted to say yes. How could she not when his kisses and caresses had been filled with a sense of urgency much stronger than ever before. He also knew she'd be surprised when he pulled away. He shook his head.

"I can't, Claire."

"I don't understand." Her eyes pleaded. "Garrett... I'm

not asking for forever. Just one night. You know I don't want you to make me any promises. I don't want anything beyond what we have. I just want you to hold me. Now. Only now. Tonight." Tears filled her eyes. "Why don't you want me?"

"That's just it, baby." He touched her cheek with the palm of his hand. "You and I both know I want you. But one night isn't enough. I need you to want this, to want me enough to say we'll try to make it last."

Her lips quivered as she held them tightly together. "Garrett, I… I'm broken. I can't be the kind of woman you need."

"What do I need?" he whispered.

"A wife who can give you children. I can't. I'm useless. I'll never be worth a damn to any man. Please, Garrett. I can't be what I'm not. Don't ask me for more than I can give."

"Oh, Claire. Who ever told you such a foolish thing?" Garrett wanted to laugh, hope soaring, but he held it in because he knew she wouldn't understand. So that's why she was holding out on him, why she refused to let their relationship advance beyond casual dating and her continued request for what he knew would spell the end because she wouldn't let it progress afterwards.

"It's why my dad took his first mistress. After my mom had me… there were complications. He blamed me for her inability to give him a son and, in his eyes, she was no longer whole. And then it happened to me… I ruined his chances for his bloodline to continue through grandchildren." She laughed bitterly. "Irony of ironies, he never fathered a child with any of those women either. None of us measured up to his expectations." She was crying full out now. Garrett's heart hurt for her. He understood why his wanting her was so important. He reached for her but she pulled away.

He didn't pursue her. Instead he told her quickly, "I don't need another child, Claire. What I need and want is *you* and for you to need and want me in return. Come to my parent's farm with me tomorrow, Claire. Please?"

She was already shaking her head. "I'm not the type you take home to meet Mum. Look at me, Garrett. I dress like a high dollar hooker, carouse as I please, live for the moment… entice innocent men into my bed." She looked at him. "I'm not good like you, Garrett."

"You're wrong, Claire. Come with me."

"No. I have to go. Goodbye, Garrett." She stepped from the car before he could protest. He didn't try to stop her even though his very being screamed for him to do so. He knew she was not in a state of reasoning. She needed time. He'd return in the morning and insist, even if it meant dragging her kicking and screaming from her fancy home. He drove off knowing it would be a long night.

# Chapter 9

Claire pushed past Charlie and headed as quickly as possible to the back hallway, just as she had when she was a little girl and life had upset her. She didn't care about the lobby occupants who watched, their mouths gaping, looks of disapproval following the grown woman in heels and bared shoulders who ran past in a whirl, knocking those who barred her path and ignoring others who tried to speak to her. All she cared about was escape, the escape she should have taken months ago.

"Fool. Idiot. You've never been able to accomplish what you've set out to do. You'll never amount to anything if that's the road you choose to follow," she chided under her breath.

Those last words were her dad's. He'd said that to her when she told him she wanted to pursue art, not college. He'd said she needed a degree. She could paint and teach or… He went nuts. Made her feel worthless; showed her again what a disappointment she'd been to him.

Why couldn't he just love her? And why couldn't Garrett just want her, stay with her sometimes, and nothing more. That way when he found someone who could give him what she couldn't, there'd be no strings attached. He could simply walk away. Why did he have to be so good?

Claire rode up the staff elevator, thankful to be alone. A perk of having been around this old building as a child, she knew the inner workings. If only she could figure out her own self as easily.

No figuring out left to do. There was too much turmoil,

too much pain. It was time to go. She wondered briefly if maybe she'd never really been meant to be.

She was calm by the time she reached her floor, her decision having been made. Undoubtedly she looked a mess and was again thankful for a vacant hall. There was only one other unit on this floor, so she wasn't surprised. Still, she was thankful. A chance encounter might deter her as it had when she'd stumbled across Garrett.

Garrett! She snorted as she clicked on the light and several of her paintings were illuminated, including the one of him as her angel. She'd left her favorites out in hopes of showing him when he finally joined her at her place. Thinking how silly she'd been to have even considered he would have come up with her that evening, she studied the paintings. There was the angel one, a farm scene with a happy family in the corner, a couple, mother and child, and the little girl she'd taken back from Old Joe not long after she'd met up with him again and asked him not to sell it.

Joe. Her heart twinged, knowing he'd be one of the few who would miss her. Pushing down her regret, she gathered the paintings into a pile in the sunroom and thrust them into an old canvas box she had in the closet. With a shaking hand, she scrawled Joe's address on the front and placed the package by the front door. Hopefully whoever found her would make sure they got to Joe. She wondered if he'd sell them or keep them. It didn't matter. At least he'd appreciate them. He was the only one who'd ever appreciated her.

Claire looked out over the city, taking in the lighted night sky. False illumination, she thought. What a hollow place; beautiful on the outside, broken on the inside. Just like her. The whole world was the same.

She went into the living room and poured herself a

Linda Boulanger

large glass of wine, kicked off her shoes right there at the bar and left them. Her dad would have been livid. All things had their place.

With a snort, she walked silently to the bedroom in her stocking feet. How anticlimactic, she thought as she opened the night stand drawer and pulled out the bottles. She reclined against the stack of silk pillows piled neatly at the headboard and studied the bottles' contents through the smoky plastic. At least they were pretty little pills, she thought, which caused her to begin to laugh hysterically, only to have the moment end in a sob. God, she was tired. She reached for the throw at the end of the bed and pulled it up over her and closed her eyes. So very, very tired.

# Chapter 10

Garrett ran a hand through his already ruffled hair and dialed Claire's number. He'd tried her three times throughout the night, praying she'd turned her phone off each time she didn't answer. By 9:30 the next morning he'd worried himself into a frenzie that had him in his car and heading toward her building.

His heart raced. He held his breath as he pulled into the circle drive and exhaled deeply, relieved when he saw the man Claire called Charlie. He'd been there the night before. Seen how upset she was. Perhaps he'd listed to reason and let him inside.

"No sir. Been on duty since 6:00. No way she could have slipped past. She's up there, sir. Just not taking your calls." The doorman raised questioning eyebrows to Garrett.

Garrett shook his head. The old man was guarded, protective. How could he convey the urgency without letting him know his fears? A quick mental rundown told him he couldn't.

"Look," he told him, "Claire was very upset last night. I'm worried she may have… she was pretty shaken and talking irrationally. I thought a good night's rest was probably best for her, but since I can't get a hold of her… I'm a psychologist. I should have known better… Can you let me in to check on her? Just to ease our minds?" he implored him.

"If you're wrong… she could have me fired on the spot." Garrett could see the concern in Charlie's eyes, knew the older gentleman was wrestling with keeping his job safe versus Claire's wellbeing. He also knew Charlie had seen how upset she was the night before and that the old guy really cared about her.

"Come on," he told Garrett, huffing out a deep breath. "Follow me."

"Thank you," Garrett said quietly on his own exhaled breath.

Charlie nodded, "Jack! I'll be right back. Cover for me, will you?" he called over to a younger man working in the lobby.

The two men were silent as they rode up the elevator. Any other time Charlie would have been filled with small talk and Garrett would have welcomed the insight into the finer details of the grand building, but not then.

Charlie fumbled with the key after their knocking provided no response. His face was washed with a mixture of both concern and relief when the lock gave way and Garrett pushed past him, then stopped.

"Which door?" he whispered and waited for Charlie to point the way.

Garrett froze at the door and closed his eyes as his heart plummeting to the pit of his stomach. The scene that hit him when he opened them – the half empty wine glass, beautiful Claire, still and lifeless, laid out on the bed with the pill bottles beside her, had his breath coming in quick, shallow gulps. He'd known, yet he'd refused to believe…

"Oh Claire," he whispered. "I'm so sorry.

The pain bottled inside for the past two and a half years surged through him. A loud guttural "No!" ripped from deep inside, startling Charlie who stared at the scene over Garrett's left shoulder. The doorman stepped back, missing Claire scurrying up and pressing against the pillows, her eyes wide in fear.

"Garrett?!" she screamed, looking around, trying to gain her bearings. Confusion reigned. She looked from a frozen Garrett to a fearful Charlie who had returned to the doorway at the sound of her voice.

Claire stiffened, her chin set as her eyes register absolute anger. "Why are you here? Either of you?" she practically growled.

Charlie began to stammer. "I'm sorry miss. You were just so upset last night. And when he suggested... I wanted to make sure you were all right. He couldn't reach you and..."

"Save it!" Claire said, the contempt in her voice thick. She shook her head.

"It's okay, Charlie," Garrett intervened.

"I told you I could lose my job over this, man!" Charlie whispered to Garrett.

"Don't worry. I'll take care of everything. Go ahead and go. You did the right thing. Thank you." Garrett's eyes never left Claire, who stared back with something akin to hatred.

"The right thing." Charlie heard her mock Garrett with his own words. "What exactly is *the right thing* Dr. O'Bryan? Is it *right* that you've disrupted my private affair? Tell me what *right* you have to be here? Do your credentials give you that *right*?"

"The fact that I care about you gives me that right," he returned calmly.

"Oh now you *care*, huh? Is that why you pushed me away last night?" she hissed.

Linda Boulanger

"Oh, Claire! Come on. I'm not the one doing the pushing." He felt his professional façade slip, a surge of anger welling up in him as he advanced toward the bed. Claire tensed, ready to scurry off the other side, then chose to stand her ground. "You've done everything you can to keep this relationship from going forward. I don't know exactly what your game is, but I'm tired of it. Now get out of that bed and get changed," he commanded.

Claire stared at him with open-mouthed disbelief. "You can't tell me what to do…"

"Then you'll go as you are." He returned her angry glare without so much as a flinch.

"And just exactly *where* am I going? Besides crazy," she mumbled the last part under her breath. "Perhaps the Looney bin?" She looked at the two bottles of pills he had picked up when he came to the edge of the bed.

"To my parents farm." His tone and his face had both softened as he too looked at the bottles.

Claire gave a sarcastic laugh as she reached for the bottles. "Those are mine," she said when he took as step back.

"Get ready, Claire," he commanded again.

"I'm not going to meet your parents on some lovely little country estate you want to call a stinking farm, so they can stare at me with that look of guarded disdain that always comes when they know their near-perfect child is on the path to making the biggest mistake of his life."

Her tone was so bitter. Garrett chose to ignore it. "Get changed," he said again, his voice icy and soft as he leaned toward her.

Claire glared at him, not moving, then shaking her head and rolling her eyes. "Oh fine! Whatever it takes to get you off my back, Mr. Psychology Man. But I'll tell you right now, this is a waste of time."

"I know. I know. Meeting parents is one step closer to commitment, and you can't commit because you have some crazy notion that you have to be able to give a man a son to count for anything. And you can't do that," he taunted as she jerked articles of clothing from their resting places in her closet and drawers. "Why exactly is it that you believe you can't?"

"Doctors." She went into the adjoining bathroom and he heard the shower water turn on. "A false positive report and an overzealous physician changed my life forever, within a few, short days."

"You didn't get a second opinion?" he asked from his position just outside the cracked door.

She didn't answer for a moment. "I was nineteen years old, Garrett. I was scared and I was stupid. My parents were away. On a trip to Africa, of all places, and I couldn't get hold of them. I didn't want to die. I was afraid to wait."

He looked down at the two pill bottles he still held. How ironic. The very thing she hadn't wanted – to die – had led her down a path to a life she no longer wanted to live. He put the bottles in his pocket, pulled out his phone, and typed a quick message to his mom.

"Well it's time you quit walking in self pity and realized there are people out there that could not only love you as you are but need you as much as you need them."

He heard her loud breath of exasperation and then muttering under her breath as the water ceased it's running. He didn't press any further, just waited, listening to the sounds of her doing all that women do to get ready. He'd missed having those sounds in his life.

The door opened fully not giving him time to delve deeper into his own thoughts. He looked her over as she emerged. He was always, *always* taken with her beauty.

"Glad you approve, though I'm sorry I'm fresh out of country couture." The water had obviously done little to wash away her annoyance.

Garrett looked down at his own clothes. "And I look like a bumpkin?" he muttered as he watched her slip into calf-height, high-heeled boots. "You're the one wearing boots."

"Very funny!" The lack of humor in her voice caused Garrett to sigh as he followed her from the room to the front door. This was going to be a long drive.

# Chapter 11

An hour and forty silent minutes later they pulled to a stop outside his parent's home. It had been a tense trip, leaving Garrett unsure Claire would even get out of the car. He watched her watching his mother when she stepped out the screen door onto the wide, wrap-around porch, her stony expression changing to one of fear and humility. Garrett resisted the urge to assure her, knowing his words would be unwelcome. Instead he got out of the car and met his mom, who had begun to come toward them.

"Hi Mom." He kissed her cheek and she patted his.

"It'll be okay," she whispered, moving past him on her way to the car. "I'm glad you're here."

Garrett didn't answer, didn't even look back until he was on the porch next to the door. Closing his eyes, he muttered a silent prayer, and waited.

Claire took a deep breath and opened the door just before Garrett's mom got to the car. She stepped out feeling completely awkward and uncomfortable in her tight fitting, low cut, designer dress, sweater, leggings, and boots. She pulled the flimsy sweater tighter about her, trying to hide what lay much deeper than just her body. Perhaps his mother wouldn't see past her outer exterior. Claire looked down and shook her head. Women had a knack for seeing inside.

Margarette O'Bryan smiled what she hoped was her most welcoming smile at the lovely creature that stepped from her son's car. She was every bit as beautiful as Garrett had said. Taking in the high-brow glamour of her clothing, Margarette thought she looked like she might have walked right out of the pages of a high dollar fashion magazine. Her heart hurt for the girl, knowing the showy exterior was a façade, though she was just as certain that deep inside there was a woman every bit as beautiful who just needed help believing herself worthy.

"You must be Claire." She extended a hand to the younger woman. "Garrett texted that he'd invited you. We're so glad you decided to come." She kept Claire's hand in hers, urging her back to the house.

Claire eyed Garrett as he held open the door, not returning his smile. She wondered how much about her he'd shared, and a new surge of self-disgust surged through her. His mother seemed so kind. She'd even held back any signs of disapproval. *Please, please*, she thought glancing up. *Please let her not hate me.*

"James? They're here." Margarette called out when they entered the house. Claire breathed in and held it for a moment. Ah yes, the father test. She glanced down at Margarette's hand, resting reassuringly on her arm, then looked up in time to see an older version of Garrett. But it wasn't the man that grabbed hold and kept her attention. It was the rather squirmy little girl he held on his hip. He tickled her and smiled as he sat her down.

"Daddy!" she shrieked, running to Garrett.

He scooped her up in his arms and smothered her with kisses, making her giggle more.

"How's my girl?" he asked, throwing a cautious glance in Claire's direction.

"Happy." She grabbed his face in her tiny hands and rubbed noses with him, then turned her cherubic face to

Claire. "Hi!"

Claire couldn't find her voice for a minute, tears clouding her vision before she finally managed to respond. "Hi," she returned quietly as Garrett's mother released her hand and nudged her gently in the direction of father and child. Claire glanced at Garrett. "Daddy?" she whispered.

He nodded. "She's all mine," he told her, his eyes never leaving hers. "Chloe, this is my friend, Claire," he told the little girl. "I've been wanting her to meet you."

Chloe held out her hands for Claire to take her. Claire hesitated, taking a couple of steadying breaths before lifting her arms and taking the child from her father. Garrett, her Garrett, was a dad. She blinked back tears as she tried the little girl's name. "Hi, Chloe."

Chloe nodded and smiled as Claire ran a hand across her silky, blonde hair. Chloe patted Claire's cheeks, studied her mass of currently dark blonde curls, then became fixated on the blue pendant around Claire's neck.

"Pretty... like you," Chloe told her, making Claire smile.

"It matches your eyes, Chloe," Claire whispered.

Seeing Claire so completely absorbed in his daughter made Garrett sigh. He looked at his mother and she inclined her head toward the living room.

"Let's go this way," Garrett quietly told Claire, taking her by the shoulders and directed her to the other room. She didn't resist, just watched Chloe continue to play with her necklace.

"There," Chloe said pointing to the big rug in front of the fireplace.

"Chloe," Garrett jumped in, "Claire may not feel comfortable on the floor..."

Linda Boulanger

"It's okay," Claire protested, putting the little girl down and lowering herself to the floor beside her. Delighted, Chloe reached for her toy basket and began to share her favorites with Claire. Garrett went to sit in one of the two big chairs across the end table from his dad, where James tried to ease his tension with general talk. Margarette went off to start their lunch, making Garrett smile when he heard her humming from the kitchen. He tried to concentrate on the conversation with his dad, but both his eyes and his attention constantly wandered back to the two in front of the fireplace.

As they played, Claire occasionally touched the tiny girl's golden hair or ran a hand down her petite arm. It was obvious she was soaking in every moment.

Chloe's little hands returned time and again to the pendant around Claire's neck.

"You like that, don't you?" Claire asked the little girl who had crawled back on her lap and sat fingering the bauble.

Chloe nodded, looked at it and then into Claire's eyes. "Your eyes. Same too."

"Sometimes," Claire agreed as the two of them stared, lost in each others eyes. "Though not as pretty as yours," she told her with a playful tap to Garrett's daughter's nose. He watched Chloe giggle and cover her nose for a second befoe removing her hand and rubbing noses with Claire. Tears swelled up in Claire's beautiful blue eyes that she worked to blink back, before giving up and pulling Chloe into a gentle hug.

"Lunch is ready," Margarette announce from the doorway. Claire glanced up, suddenly embarrassed. She'd been so completely mesmerized by Garrett's beautiful little girl that she'd nearly forgotten the others.

"Chloe girl, I'll race you to the sink," James told his granddaughter. "Let's get washed up." Chloe bounced up quickly and ran from the room with James in her wake.

Claire watched them go, then looked up at Garrett. He held out his hand and she took it, allowing him to help her up. Standing in front of him, Claire fought back more unwanted, unexplained tears.

"Come here," he told her, pulling her into his arms.

"Why didn't you tell me?" she whispered against his chest as he stroked her hair.

"I wanted you to see her first." He shrugged. "I guess I was afraid…" He tipped her chin up to him. "I thought if you met her… maybe you'd realize we need you." He kissed her. "I've fallen in love with you, Claire. With *you*, just the way you are. I think we compliment each other pretty well with what we have to offer. I think it's a pretty good fit." He paused for a moment. "Will you let us in?" He placed his hand over her heart. "Both of us?"

The tears that welled in Claire's eyes continued to make their way down her cheeks. Her lips trembling, she told him, "I wanted to let you in for a long time now. But I was so scared." She studied him, her eyes boring into his. "You really mean that, Garrett? You really want me? Knowing I can't…"

Garrett silenced her with his fingers to her lips. "You're perfect, Claire. Just the way you are. She pulled in a long, quivering breath, her hand coming up to cover her chest. She closed her fingers over her pendant. Looking down, Garrett smiled and touched the bauble in her hand. "Pretty," he told her. "Like you." The laugh they shared dissolved as he lowered his head to hers and kissed her … a slow kiss, filled with promises. "We'd better get in to lunch

Linda Boulanger

before they send out a search party in the form of a two and a half year old," he whispered when he pulled back, resting his forehead against hers. Claire nodded and slid her arm down to his waist.

They walked from the room arm in arm causing both Garrett's parents to beam in approval when they entered the kitchen.

"Sit here, Claire." Chloe pointed to the chair next to her. "Okay Daddy?"

"Of course." He pulled out the chair for Claire, then went to sit on the other side of the table, across from his two girls.

# Chapter 12

Chloe seemed reluctant to let Claire move very far away from her after her daddy announced it was almost time for them to leave.

"You will come back?" she asked, clinging to Claire's hand.

"I'd love to come back, Chloe, and hopefully soon." Claire squatted down and placed her hands on Chloe's tiny waist. She wanted desperately to reassure the little girl, wished she could tell her it wouldn't be long before Garrett took her and Chloe to live with him as a family. But what if she'd misunderstood his intentions when they were standing in front of the fireplace in his parents' living room?

"You sure?" Chloe must have sensed Claire's reservations. Her little lips trembled when she asked.

"Cross my heart." It was an assurance she'd received often from her own mother. Her finger caught on the pendant chain as she made the criss-cross on her chest. Reaching up, she removed the necklace, refastened it, and slipped it over the blonde-topped head. Making a display of positioning it, she smiled at a very wide-eyed Chloe. "Will you watch this for me until I come back?"

Chloe nodded as she fingered the bauble. "Gram! Look!" She held it up for Margarette to see.

"Come show me, Baby." Margarette held out her hands and Chloe scurried away, giving Claire the opportunity to finish getting ready to leave.

She looked up to see Garrett staring at her. "You don't have to do that, Claire. I know what your pendant means to you," he whispered. "She'll be fine."

Claire nodded and smiled. "I know. Just make sure you bring me back for it." She looked down at Chloe who had joined them again. "It's my assurance too, I hope."

"That's a promise," he told her, squeezing her hand before swinging Chloe up into his arms and handing her to Margarette.

"Bye, Daddy." Chloe kissed him as he hugged his mother and his child. "Call me."

"Every day. Just like always." They rubbed noses.

"Claire, thank you for coming. Our door is always open," James told her, stepping up to open the screen.

"Thank you. It was my pleasure. I'm already looking forward to the next time." Claire looked from James to Margarette with gratitude. She blew a kiss to Chloe as Garrett ushered her out the door.

After about fifteen minutes of silence, Garrett cut his eyes in Claire's direction and sighed. "This isn't going to be like it was on the way up, is it? That was a really long trip."

Claire had been staring out her widow. She turned to look at him. "How can you bear to leave her?"

Garrett didn't say anything at first, trying to find the words to explain what he felt in his heart. "I love her enough to know she needs more than I can give her by myself. What kind of life would that be for her with me in the city? Spending the better part of her days with a sitter of some sort so I could satisfy my desire for a few short hours with her every evening? I want her with me, Claire, more than anything. But not without the right woman to share our lives." He looked at Claire then continued with added emphasis on his words. "Did you hear what I said? Not just *any* woman - the *right* woman."

Another glance in Claire's direction showed her thoughts plainly displayed on her face. Forehead wrinkled, eyes brimming with unshed tears, she held her lips tightly clenched. They turned down at the corners, even while she tried to control their quivering. Garrett knew the same fears still plagued her. Her inability to have children was still there. The pain embedded by the years of rejection by her father hadn't lessened. He reached for her hand.

"I'm satisfied with what I have, Claire. I don't need a son to make me whole. I want a good life for my daughter, and the woman I love." He paused. "I'd like to see you as a contented part of that life. Besides," he gently squeezed her hand a couple of times, "I could attempt to fill a house full of children and there'd be no guarantee I'd ever have a son anyway. I'm happy with what I've been given. I'd rather spend my time helping others and knowing that gift is what makes me live on. Not my name or my blood line. People that can't see beyond their own selfish desires are not happy people, Claire. I don't want to live my life lamenting with what I can't do or don't have. I want to enjoy what I do and spread that joy to others who need it."

Claire was silent again, thought Garrett didn't mind this time. He knew she was thinking over all he'd said, all she'd thought her life could be, and what it might be now. "You really are an earthly angel," she whispered.

He laughed and brought her hand to his lips, kissing the back of her fingers. "So you'll let me replace your mother's rings with a set of your own? No more doubts?"

She nodded, then bit her lower lip, her eyes shifting down.

"But?" he asked, sensing her hesitation.

Claire didn't answer at first. Something wasn't right. Not once had anyone mentioned Chloe's mom. How was she going to figure into this picture? Claire was fearful enough. She wasn't sure she could compete with a woman who could do what she couldn't. Her fear was too deeply rooted.

Certain she didn't want to know the answer, but knowing she needed to, Claire asked quietly, "Where's Chloe's mom, Garrett?"

Claire watched the muscles in his neck tighten, saw him fighting to swallow. He shook his head. Claire wasn't sure if that meant he didn't know or he wasn't going to answer her. Then he began to talk.

"Elaine and I had been married for five years when she got pregnant with Chloe. She'd finished her education and my practice was just starting to really take off. She loved the society life of the city, having grown up a mid-western country girl. Life seemed golden. The timing was perfect, so I thought." He pulled in a ragged breath and continued, "She was sick a lot during the pregnancy and when the constant barrage of parties and activities practically ceased all together, she got depressed. I was so deliriously happy about our baby that I didn't see just how deep she was spiraling. Or maybe I didn't want to see. I convinced myself that what she was battling was normal, figured it would pass. I tried to cheer her up instead of helping her, talking incessantly about how grand it would be once the baby came." He laughed, a low hollow sound, and shook his head. "One day she yelled at me to shut up about the stupid baby, telling me how her life was ruined. She believed all her hopes and dreams were over, told me that she didn't want to be saddled with taking care of my brat for the rest of her life."

"Oh Garrett. How... Hadn't you discussed children? Wasn't Chloe planned?"

"Yes, she'd talked the talk of wanting a house full of children. And maybe if she'd gotten her fill of social climbing before she'd gotten pregnant it would have been different. Chloe wasn't planned. But five years... the timing seemed right." He shrugged.

"Where's Elaine now? No one mentioned her today, not even Chloe. When does she see her daughter? Why doesn't Chloe live with her?" Claire dared to ask.

Garrett sighed and was quiet again for a few minutes before he began. "When Chloe was three weeks old she asked me to take the baby to my parents' for the weekend. She said she was tired and needed the rest. It seemed reasonable. My parents were elated to have us, and Chloe was like another child under my mom's care. She cooed when Mom talked to her, followed her with her eyes, and didn't sleep nearly as much. That's when I realized just how lifeless she'd been. I know I should have known, but I didn't know a lot about newborns and maybe I didn't want to admit to what was going on right under my own roof." He shrugged, his face remained somber, not softening at all when he smiled. "I'd really wanted to believe my baby's lack of interaction was normal, and had actually disillusioned myself. That's when my concern for Elaine's true state couldn't stay hidden" He rubbed his face as he looked out the window. "I fought my fears all through the night, working and reworking what we needed to do to get our lives back together. But, when I couldn't reach her by phone the next morning, I told my mom I needed to go."

He breathed deeply, trying to retain control over his emotions. The tension on his face told Claire this memory was one he'd worked hard to suppress. "Our unit was still quiet when I entered and I full well expected to find it empty with a Dear John note propped against my pillow just like you see in the movies."

"But you didn't?" Claire prodded when he didn't go on.

He shook his head. Tears welled in his eyes. "Claire, when I walked into your apartment this morning and saw you laying on your bed with the wine glass on the night stand and the pill bottles on the bed... I felt as if I'd walked back in time."

Claire's hands flew up to cover her mouth. "Oh my God," she whispered, feeling as if she'd been punched in the heart.

"Only the scene was not pristine and pretty. She was a mess. Her hair was snarled, her face sunken. She'd put on ratty old pajamas, thrown up all over the bed, and died. There was no happy ending for her, and I blamed myself. I should have known."

The quiet tears that ran down Claire's cheeks broke Garrett's heart. He knew they were for all of them – her, him, Chloe, even Elaine and all they'd been through. He felt tears stinging his own eyes and blinked them away.

"I'm sorry," she said, her voice cracking. "I'm so sorry, Garrett.

Sorry that happened to you, and sorry it all came back to you this morning." He nodded, not expecting her to continue, though she did. "But I'm not sorry you found me and that you firmly stood up and made me go with you to your parents'. You've saved my life twice, Garrett. Did you know that?"

He looked at her, his brows rising in surprise.

"The night I took your table at the restaurant... that

was to be my last meal. I'd planned to indulge then go home and end it all, because I hated who I'd become. But you made me give my word that we'd share Sunday brunch."

"I remember. I asked if you were truly a woman of your word. I'd been afraid to let you go that night…" Realization lit his face. "Claire, when I talked to Chloe that evening before leaving for my date she said the strangest thing. She told me to say hi to her mommy for her. I laughed and brushed it off as silly kid talk. Boy! I really need to quit brushing things off."

Quiet laughter echoed from them both as they each retreated into reflective thought.

"What is this place?" Claire asked when they passed back by a grand, gated entrance with a big for sale sign on it. It had caught her attention on the way up as well, though her anger had made her refuse to ask.

"It's an old boarding stable. It needs some work but it's a great place with solid bones. My dad had dreams of buying it, actually running it after retirement."

Claire looked at him from beneath scrunched brows. "Why didn't he?" she asked.

Garrett sighed. "He gave up that dream for a new one named Chloe. They knew I'd need help with her, so he took early retirement and put their investment into the farm and making ends meet to help me take care of her. He's told me time and again that she's the joy of their old age and everything they gave up has been replaced by something far more valuable."

"What will they do once you take her? Do you think he'll buy the stables then?" she pressed.

Garrett shook his head. "I don't think they have the means now. Early retirement took its toll. Then the purchase of the farm. He's figured everything out to where they'll live okay, though not extravagantly. Perhaps a trip or two. But certainly no horse ranches."

Claire didn't answer beyond a nod, and they lapsed into easy silence, each again with inner thoughts.

"Garrett?" Her voice breaking the silence made him jump. "Are you tied to having your practice in the city? I mean, I assume you want to continue working in some capacity, although you do realize you wouldn't have to."

Garrett frowned. "I'm not following you here, not sure what you're saying at all."

She laughed, her eyes were filled with excitement and anticipation.

Garrett raised a brow. "Something tells me you're hatching a plan." They both laughed and she began to run her idea by him. His eyes were shining as brightly as hers when she finished.

"You'd really do that, Claire?" Garrett asked, gratitude and love shining in his eyes. "I think it's perfect... for all of us."

She smiled at him, her expression turning dreamy when he reached for her hand and brought it to his lips.

# Chapter 13

"What time is it?" Claire asked as they neared her building.

Garrett looked at his watch, both of them seeming oblivious to the clock in the car dash. "A little before 5:00. Why?"

"Keep going. I want you to meet someone -- the old artist I was telling you about."

Garrett looked skeptical.

*Please*, Claire thought. *Don't start in now, telling me all the reasons this dream won't fly. Don't dash my hopes. Please…*

Garrett shrugged. "You sure he won't mind? If he closes at five…"

"For us he'll be open, and it's only a couple blocks down." With a broad smile spreading across her face, Claire leaned over and kissed his cheek.

Chuckling, and with a smile that matched hers, Garrett asked her what the kiss was for.

"For not saying no. For letting me dream."

"It's a nice dream, Claire. I like the idea of dreaming it with you."

Claire rested her head against the back of the seat and sighed. Acceptance was a wonderful feeling.

Jerking forward, she pointed to an empty parking space and told Garrett to stop, relaxing again when he pulled in. They'd almost missed it. Before she could release the door handle she'd just reached for, Garrett grabbed her other arm. "Claire." He struggled for a couple of seconds with what he had to say. "From here on, we walk forward as a team, okay?" Even with Claire's brows furrowed instead of her agreeing, he continued. "If we want to make this work… not just the dream, but us also… we have to. It doesn't mean we'll always agree, but we have to be willing to see the other's side in everything. I need you to remember, to believe your ideas and dreams are just as important as mine. That may mean one of us altering course from time to time, but if we love each other, we'll do that." He stared at her until she finally nodded. "You've got a lot of good inside you. You just need to believe it. I'll help you and you can do the same for me."

"Okay," she agreed, nodding again, and then kissing him. "I love you, Garrett," she whispered. It was the first time she could ever remember saying these words to a man.

Garrett's smile widened as he pulled back, just in time to see the sign flipping. "Looks like someone's closing up shop."

Claire turned to see Old Joe's shadow fading behind the glass on the door. She pushed out of the car and hustled to the door where she began to knock. "Joe! It's Claire," Garrett heard her call. Seconds later the door opened and the pudgy old man embraced the slender young woman. Claire looked back and motioned for Garrett to follow.

"So you brought your angel to meet me?" he ventured.

"What makes you think he's the angel?"

"Two angels go together." His smile broadened when Garrett joined them and slipped his hand over Claire's. "And the old man from your building brought the paintings. They all sold today. Quickly too. Though I pulled two thinking you must have sent them by mistake. I'll get them for you." He shuffled off to bring back the paintings. When he returned, he laid the one the one of Garrett with his angel wings on the table first, and Garrett's surprised laughter filled the room.

"I look pretty good in all white," he joked. "Amazing work, Claire. Subject aside. I'm impressed. And the other?" he asked Joe, his eagerness to see more palpale in the way his eyes shined and in his inability to stand still.

Claire gasped when Joe turned over the second painting and it was the one of the little girl. She watched Garrett trace a finger over the child's face, whose likeness was so close to Chloe's that it couldn't be denied. Claire couldn't hide the tears that began to slide down her cheeks.

Garrett pulled her into his arms and, with a shaky voice, she explained. "Many years ago, I told Old Joe that was a portrait of my little girl. I didn't realize until now how much she looks like Chloe," Claire whispered. "My heart knew…" She turned her head so that she could see Joe. He nodded.

"I don't know who Chloe is, but I've always said there are things the heart knows long before we do."

They filled him in on their lives; their plans to marry, Chloe, the dream. Then Claire asked him if he'd be willing to join their forces and what part he would play. The couple got ready to leave with the assurance they'd return soon with details.

"Thanks for being there for her," Garrett whispered to Joe as they clasped hands.

The old man nodded. "It was mutual. We needed each other. She was my earthly angel. She saved me from uncertainty. I merely pushed her to perfect her talent and let her know somebody cared. We all need that, along with opportunities to pursue our dreams. You two have come up with a great idea. And you have an amazing woman by your side for this venture. I know you know that, but I'll keep reminding you of it from time to time." Joe chuckled.

"I do know it, but I don't mind being told," Garrett assured him.

Joe clapped him on the back and shooed him to the curb where Claire was loading the two paintings into the back seat of his car.

# Chapter 14

Three months later Claire and Garrett pulled up in front of Garrett's parent's home. Margarette laughed as an overly excited Claire bound from the car. Her attempt at country attire still looked like high-dollar fashion with her tight jeans tucked inside her red western boots, upscale black and red plaid shirt tied at the waist with a red lace camisole peaking from the neckline.

"Nice piggy tails," she teased her almost daughter-in-law when they embraced

"Thanks," Claire laughed. "Someday I'll get it right."

"Oh I sure hope not. I think you're perfect just the way you are," Margarette told her and they hugged again.

James came around from the back, pulled by an exuberant Chloe who was actually bouncing in place with excitement over seeing her daddy and Claire.

"It's not Saturday," she told them, running up to Claire.

"Nope. But we have a surprise." She scooped Chloe up and hugged her tightly.

Margarette raised her brows and looked at Claire's left hand.

"No, we didn't sneak away and secretly get married." Claire assured her. They all laughed and Garrett snapped his fingers, trying to assume a commanding posture.

"Quickly," he told them, pointing to the car as Claire started herding them in that direction.

Margarette raised her eyebrows when Claire opened the back door to reveal a seat for Chloe already secured in the middle.

Claire's smile was tentative. "We'll need it eventually," she said almost apologetically when she climbed in on the other side and watched Margarette buckle Chloe in.

"And what a joyous day that will be," Margarette said. "Children should be raised by their parents and spoiled mercilessly by their grandparents - which cannot be done properly when they live under the same roof." The two women laughed. Margarette reached for her hand and gave it a squeeze. Claire was thinking how she was as thankful for Margarette as she was for Garrett when she heard James say something about the old stables. Her oversized smile and bouncing knees were a clear indication of just how excited she was.

"Yes, I heard," Garrett answered vaguely when his dad said the place had sold. He glanced in the mirror at Claire. "You're as bad as a child at Christmas," he told her reflection.

"I didn't say anything!" She giggled.

"What are you two up to?" Margarette looked from her son to Claire, then to Chloe and shrugged. The little shoulders raised and fell, mimicking her grandmother, and they all laughed.

Garrett eased the car into the stables' driveway. The iron gates were already open and they could see several work crews milling about in various places on the property.

"Should we be here?" James asked, receiving no answer as Garrett got out of the car.

"Help me. Will you, Dad?" Garrett said before shutting his door. James glanced back at Claire who was trying without success to contain an ear to ear smile.

"Go. Go!" she told him before turning to unbuckle Chloe. "You too." She motioned for Margarette to get out as well.

Working at the rope that held the heavy tarp in place over the new sign, Garrett pulled the know free and the material fell free to reveal the barely dried painting of the barns and horses in the meadow. The name stood out distinctly in the blue sky. "Welcome to O'Bryan Meadows," it read. "A place where dreams are allowed to grow."

"What is this?" James asked.

"It's going to be a place where we bring kids that need a little help in understanding they truly do make a difference -- a place where they can explore passions like art and horseback riding, cooking, all sorts of things beyond the uppity professions their parents are trying to force them into," Claire blurted out, her voice rising in excitement. "My daddy's name and money may not have helped me, but there's no reason it can't help others... kids like me whose family standing and money can buy them everything but happiness. I've been doing some research..." She looked at Garrett. "*We've* been looking into the statistics, and it's alarming the number of wealthy families who have lost children to suicide because those kids either felt unloved or couldn't handle the lives they were expected to live." She turned to James. "We were hoping you might oversee the stables."

James looked from Claire to Garrett then down at the ground. He had to clear his throat twice before he could speak. "This old place has been a dream of mine for years. I never could figure it out in my mind how it could pay for itself... or even how to pay for it in the first place." They all laughed. He looked over the place then at the sign. "You two have really thought this through? You know what you're getting into?"

Claire, wrapped in Garrett's arms, looked up at him. "I

don't know about Garrett but I don't have a clue." There was even more laughter. "But you know what they say? It's not what you know, but who. We've enlisted the help of a lot of people who are considered experts. And I know a couple of old gents who see these kids day in and day out… they're already working on a list of those who need our help."

"We're buying the old Miller place too," Garrett added. "We won't be taking Chloe too far away, and it looks like we'll be working together in a roundabout sort of way," he told his dad. "I know it's not quite as good as owning it yourself, but…"

"Nope," James interrupted. "It's better. I can't think of a better use for this place." He looked at Claire again, moisture making his eyes glisten. "You know you're an angel, don't you, Claire?"

She was already shaking her head before his words faded. "Not me. But I've had my share to help me along the way." She looked up at Garrett and he kissed her. "I want others to have that same opportunity."

"Horses!" Chloe squealed pointing to a nearby pasture.

"Yes Chloe. *Our* horses. Want to go and see?" Garrett asked her. She nodded her head and squealed again. "Come on, Grandpa," Garrett said to his dad. "Let's go check out your charges." He kissed Claire's head and handed her the car keys before jogging off to catch up with his dad and Chloe.

Claire looked at the keys and bit her lower lip, "Margarette, I don't know how to drive," she confessed in a quiet, monotone voice. Living most of her life in the city, she'd never needed to learn.

"Guess you'd best learn if you're planning to live out here. No time like the present." She chuckled and climbed into the passenger side of the car.

"Uh, Garrett. Has Claire ever driven a car before," James asked after looking over his shoulder.

"I... huh, I don't know. Why?" He straightened from the squatted position he'd used to look through the fence with Chloe.

"Well, I'm pretty sure your future wife's getting her first driving lesson." James inclined his head toward the car that kept easing forward and then stopping only to begin again.

Garrett's brows came down toward his eyes.

"Daddy's mad?" Chloe's voice was filled with childish concern.

"No. No, Baby. I'm not." He smiled to assure her. "Just realizing there's a lot about a beautiful lady with a huge heart that I really don't know."

James chuckled. "You may never know all about her, son. That's part of the beauty of women. They're like a sweet, special surprise that reveals itself little by little each and every day."

The two men embraced and began to walk toward the main building that would house the social activities of the operations. Claire and Margarette had safely arrived and were waiting inside.

Garrett grabbed Claire when they walked in and hugged her tightly. He was suddenly overwhelmed with gratitude that Donna had canceled and Mr. Ballard had mistakenly given his table away. He realized that sometimes in life it seemed like you were losing when, in fact, you were being positioned to win bigger than you could ever imagine possible.

He knew life with Claire would be filled with the

unexpected. His future wife was uniquely wonderful, both inside and out. He smiled down at her. Was finding her a lucky break... or fate? Either way, Garrett knew he was right where he was supposed to be -- encircled in hope, found only in the arms of his angel.

# Bonus Section:

Enjoy two short stories
with ties to *Arms of an Angel*

## *Life Changes*
©2013 by Linda Boulanger

Chloe choked down a swallow of coffee and reached for the ringing phone.

"Hello!" Although the caller received her greeting, her eyes and attention remained on the computer screen before her. Who'd have thought organizing her artwork on her website would be such a difficult task? She certainly hadn't or she wouldn't have left it to the last minute. Tomorrow she had to forward the link for the new pages to a potential buyer in Paris. *Paris!* Chloe barely stifled a squeal at the thought that a Paris gallery wanted to see her artwork. If they chose to represent her, life would never be the same.

Her brain finally turned to the call, registering the silence on the other end. A deep crease etched into the porcelain expanse between her drawn eyebrows. "Hello? May I help you?" she asked, attempting to keep felt concern from tainting her voice. Maybe it was the Paris gallery with a bad connection. She waited a couple more seconds before continuing. "Is…anyone there?"

"Chloe. It's Matt. Matt Hanson."

Chloe's breath caught, her heart pounding beneath the form hugging cashmere sweater that so perfectly matched the pink tint of her glossed lips. Matt. As if she'd need his last name to know the voice that had haunted her dreams for the past five years. Her mind was already whirling, filling with questions – the main one being why her ex-husband's right hand man was calling her. The second centered around the butterflies taking flight in her belly at the sound of his voice.

There was something else... that undeniable sense of dread that accompanies an unexpected call.

"Matt. It's been a long time. Is... is everything okay?" That was Chloe, never one to beat around the bush. On most things, anyway. Her stomach tightened when Matt sighed and began to answer with halting words.

"I... I'm ... Ah Chloe..." There was another moment of silence before he blurted out, "It's James..." Chloe noted the deep timbre of his voice held a definite mournful tone.

"What's happened, Matt? Where's James? Is he okay? Tell me he's okay!" Chloe's voice rose with the last sentence, tears filling her blue eyes. She may not be married to James anymore, but she still cared, loved him in fact. Just not the kind of love needed to make a marriage work. Not the way she loved... She shook her head, pushed a hand into her blond hair and leaned forward to where her elbows rested on the desk before her. She pressed the phone tighter against her ear. "Matt?"

"It's not good, Chloe. He rolled his truck down that hill by the curve about a mile from the house..."

She hadn't been there in years, yet Chloe knew the exact spot Matt was describing, knew it could be dangerous when the roads were bad if someone didn't know the road. But James knew that road, knew to be careful. What had happened? She thought of all the times he'd talked about having it reworked to lessen the danger. Obviously he never had.

Matt's words jarred her back to the unwanted news. "Doc Wilson... He said I'd better call you." He cleared his throat. Did that sniffling sound in the receiver mean Matt was crying?

"I'll let you know my flight information," she told him, tears beginning to roll down her cheeks.

"Chloe?"

"Yes?"

"Get here quickly."

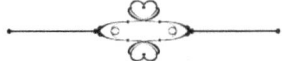

The beeping in Chloe's ear let her know another call was coming in. She went straight from the devastating news about James to talking to her mom. Step mom, actually, though she was the only mother Chloe had ever known and she loved her as much as a true flesh and blood parent.

"Can you be at the airport in forty-five minutes, Chloe?" Claire hadn't even inquired as to how her daughter was or whether she wanted to make the trip. Chloe's get-to-the-point attitude was definitely *inherited*.

"I'm not sure. I... How did you know, Mom?" Her mind hadn't cleared from that initial moment when she first heard Matt's voice, mere thought and decisions becoming more difficult with the growing muddle.

"You're still listed as James' next of kin. Sheriff Dailey called to see if we would get hold of you and I figured when your line rang through to voicemail you were talking to Matt." The two women were both silent for a moment, each no doubt lost in her own thoughts. "I've already contacted Tom Miller. You remember Tom? He stayed here at The Meadows maybe six, seven years ago.

His dream was to be a pilot even though his daddy wanted to steer him toward the helm of the company business. Investments brokerage, I think. Anyway, he flies private charters now and said he'd be waiting for you at the airport."

"But how'd you know I would agree to come?" Chloe choked out through her tears.

"I never doubted it for a second."

In her mind, Chloe could see an understanding smile turn Claire's lips upward. It was the same smile she used on the kids who spent time at O'Bryan Meadows – a place of exploration for privileged kids with dashed hopes of being able to live their own dreams instead of being molded into what their parents wanted for them. It was a place born out of Claire's life as a wealthy yet unhappy young woman, made to feel completely useless and unwanted by a father who couldn't see what a wonderful daughter he had because she didn't fit his ideal mold. Claire had almost taken her own life, just as Chloe's biological mother had. Only Elaine O'Bryan had succeeded. Chloe shivered. She longed to have Claire's gentle arms wrapped tightly around her just as they had been that night she explained why she had to leave James.

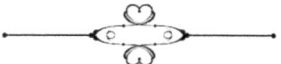

Chloe's dad, always analyzing/overly doting, met her at the top of the narrow steps as the door to the plane let down. He pulled her into a smothering hug before pushing her back so he could look at her.

"I'm all right, Daddy." Her red rimmed eyes and the tissues that had piled high during the hour and a half trip told a different story, but Garrett O'Bryan, gracious man that he was, chose to go along with Chloe's self-assessment.

"Let's get to the car so we can get you where you need to be. Claire managed to get clearance to bring it right up here. I don't know how she does it but I swear that woman can accomplish anything."

Chloe smiled at her dad's nervous prattle and obvious pride in his wife's capabilities. A stroke of pain sliced through her heart at the thought of her parents' love for one another. It was something she longed for and one of the main reasons she'd left James. She had hoped to move on and find what her parents shared.

Only what she'd wanted was back at James McCormick's Kentucky horse ranch.

With a great deal of effort, she pushed the thought away and followed Garrett down the plane's steps, glad her feet were back on solid ground. Flying had certainly never been a dream she'd harbored. Claire was waiting for her, standing beside the pilot, just a few steps away. Catching sight of her unleashed the flood of tears Chloe tried to hold back. Oh how they flowed, especially once she was in Claire's arms.

With a barely audible Thank You to Tom, Claire steered her to the waiting car and climbed into the back seat beside her. She pulled Chloe close, nestling the younger woman in her arms just as she'd done every time Chloe had ever needed her.

Chloe gasped causing Matt to turn toward the door. He'd been slumped forward in the chair beside James' bed, his head bent, hand wrapped around that of his friend. It was one of those moments that would be forever imprinted in her mind. She covered her mouth with her hand to smother a sob as he rose and started toward her. It wasn't until she was wrapped in his arms, pressed against him, that she let out a shaky breath.

Never had anything felt so wonderful and so awful at the same time as it did standing in James' hospital room in Matt's arms. The dull, gray-blue setting, meant to soothe, heightened her senses to the shadow of sickness and death, as did the sounds of the equipment monitoring James' vitals. Yet breathing in Matt's woodsy scent, melting into the security that came with having him hold her... Why did being near him always feel so right, even when she knew it was wrong?

"He's been asking for you." Matt loosened his hold – just enough for her to lean back so he could easily see her face. She saw the wariness in Matt's eyes at the hope within her own. "He fades in and out. Mostly he's out." He closed his eyes for a moment leaving Chloe to wonder what he was hiding. "They've got him so doped up … Doc called it 'keeping him comfortable.' Says that's all they can do."

Chloe shook her head, her eyes filling with tears.

"Shhh." A thumb dashed away the single drop that managed to escape to roll down her cheek. "We have to be strong – for James and for each other, okay?"

Chloe nodded, her lips quivering as she tried to smile.

"I'm glad you're here. James will be too," he whispered to her.

Unsure how to answer, she turned to a different line of conversation, though still on James. Otherwise she'd have to say she didn't want to be there, didn't want to face death or what she'd run away from almost five years ago. "I don't understand how this could have happened. He knew those roads, Matt. How could he have misjudged that turn?"

Matt turned his face away, gazing off at a vacant spot on the icy blue wall for so long Chloe was sure he wasn't going to answer, not that she'd really expected him to. Hows and Whys were never fully explained in life events.

He sighed loudly, tightened his hold, closing the distance between them. "Driving too fast. Distracted by..."

"By?" She didn't like the way he seemed to be dancing around without answering her.

He rolled his shoulders and his neck as if he was getting ready for a fight. "I suppose there's no reason to hide the truth from you now. But you need to remember something. You have to know that James loved you."

She nodded. She did know. That was why she'd left, left both men instead of coming between them and their thicker-than-blood friendship. She'd done that because she loved him.

"When we were in college there was this girl... Amy Cole." Chloe watched him travel back in time. "She ran with a pretty wild crowd, liked to party, and liked what she saw in the way of a future with James McCormick."

"What does this have to do wi..."

Matt placed a finger to her lips and continued. "When Amy turned up pregnant and swore the baby was his, James' parents stepped in and said no. You might remember Bart McCormick already had James' straight-backed, soft leather chair waiting in the office next to his."

She remembered James coming to O'Bryan Meadows. A young college sophomore, he was actually older than most of their guests, so after Claire met him she hired him as a summer employee. She'd then made sure part of his duties would have him sitting in on the sessions that would benefit him the most.

"Bart told James he'd work out an agreement to help

support the child if James would walk away. If not, he'd disown him and neither he nor the child would have anything."

"Was the baby his?" Chloe wasn't sure she wanted to know and yet had to.

"I honestly don't know. I'm sure it was possible." He looked almost apologetic. "We were young college boys, you know." Finger to forehead, he closed his eyes for a moment. "He looks an awful lot like James, Chloe."

Looks... He'd seen him? "You've seen him?"

"After James' dad died Amy called the ranch. Seems old Bart hadn't made provisions for after his death. I'm not sure I fully understand it, but James wanted to try to forge a relationship with the boy, a son who didn't even know or care that he existed until he convinced Amy to relocate to Clearview."

Chloe tried to process all she was hearing. The one thing she understood was why James had wanted to know his son. He'd wanted them to start a family right away. Chloe hadn't been ready, knew the marriage was a farce on her end. Now, guilt grabbed her. She'd denied him, even knowing the depth of his desire to be the father to his own child that his father never was to him. She tried to calculate the boy's age.

"He's fifteen," Matt answered as if he'd read her mind. "He has a lot of... issues." He ignored Chloe's raised eyebrows and continued. "I don't know what happened, Chloe, but James was on his way back from Clearview when he ran off the road. There's something else. Amy was with him. She died on impact."

"Where's their son?"

Matt was about to answer when her name floated to them, a raspy whisper from across the room.

Chloe and Matt both moved to the bedside. "I'm here, James." She spoke softly, leaning down so he could hear her, maybe feel her.

His eyes were muddy, lids heavy, though he managed to open them long enough to look at her. His bruised and cracked lips tried to form a smile.

"I'm a mess," he croaked.

"You always were, cowboy," she answered, squeezing his hand before slipping into the chair where Matt had sat.

"I'm glad you came." His words were broken, just like his body.

"You knew I would." A tear slid down her cheek.

He opened his eyes again, looking in Matt's direction before closing them again. "You told her about Robbie."

"Yeah," Matt answered.

"He's a good boy. Needs to know that." He squeezed Chloe's hand in a silent plea, his whole body tightening while he fought for shallow breaths of air. "So tired, Chloe."

"Just rest, James. Everything will be okay."

James nodded and turned his face away.

I know someday I will be thankful for this moment, she thought as she watched the shallowness of his breath increase until he took his last. Though for now she could feel only numbness seeping in. So many secrets. So many words left unsaid. Bending toward his hand within hers, she kissed the wedding ring he still wore and tasted the saltiness of her tears there. How would she ever get through this?

Matt's hand covered hers and James'. His arm around her shoulder, she leaned into him. Had it only been a few hours ago that she'd been dreaming of Paris?

Life would never be the same.

# Healing Words

## ©2013 by Linda Boulanger

Sam released the handle of the hospital room door, his fingertips slipping from the cold metal with the realization he had no business being there. Sure, he was a doctor. Yes, he'd performed the medical procedures in the operating room that had most likely saved the life of the patient inside.

*And changed it dramatically.*

His heart hurt knowing hers would when she finally awakened to find the tiny life inside her gone. Damn, he'd hated to do that, but the bleeding… Car wreck victims were never easy to treat, though he'd bet a week of his physicians' salary that part of this young woman's trauma was suffered well before she'd wrapped her little car around a tree three days prior.

Sam had visited her room every day since, hoping for news she'd awakened, knowing there was no medical reason she had not.

*Except a reason to want to.*

That thought made him wonder if somehow she already knew about the baby, about the fact that she'd never have the chance to carry another one. Day and night since he'd treated her in the ER thoughts about her had plagued him. What was her story? What had she been through? And the worst: had her wreck been an accident?

No. He refused to believe she'd intentionally ran off the road into the shallow ravine, her car rolling twice before bending in half when it was stopped by the thick trunk of a tall tree. But if she'd been speeding, her tears mixed with the rain … visibility would have been limited, control lessened. What was her story?

Sam shook his head. He shouldn't care. Being impassionate, impersonal was Med 101. Getting involved in a patient's life was simply not allowed.

"Everything okay, Doc?"

Sam turned toward the gently inquiring voice, returned the smile she offered him, knowing her age-wisened eyes missed nothing. She didn't ask why he was there. Perhaps she knew the reason even better than he did.

He nodded and ran a hand through the dark hair cropped short on his head before sucking in a deep breath to answer.

"You haven't been in yet, then." Wanda Velory, the head nurse of Dana Covey Women's Hospital spoke before he did. "No change, though she's doing just fine thanks to your handiwork." She paused then shook her head. "Still no visitors. Pretty, young thing like her, you'd think her room would be full. At least she will be once the scrapes and bruises heal." She looked off into the distance before continuing, "Makes no sense, really."

She'd voiced his thoughts. "What about her parents? Or…the baby's father?"

Wanda shook her graying head. "Not a word. Haven't even inquired about how she's doing. None of them. Parents were notified. Boyfriend, it seems, is nowhere to be found." She was watching him again, imploring him with those gray-blue eyes. "Not very often that I recommend getting involved, Sam. I know it goes against all our medical training, but I have a feeling she could sure use a friend and I'm guessing you could too. You've done nothing but work since Laura left…"

"That's not true!" he interrupted, his lips thinning into a tight line. "What about my girls?"

Wanda chuckled and shook her head again. "Don't take offense, Hon. But they're six and four. Dinner dates at McDonalds with your daughters a couple of nights a week isn't exactly what I meant. That kind of interaction and socializing isn't the only thing you need and we both know it. You're looking for something, Sam. Even if you don't want to fess up to it." She smiled, not the smile of one who has caught someone else with his hand in the candy jar, but a compassionate, understanding upturning of the lips. "What do you think keeps drawing you back here?" She patted the firmness of his upper bicep, covered by the starched white dress shirt usually hidden beneath a knee length doctor's coat. "Perhaps the attention of a new friend would help Emma wake up."

*Emma.* Not just a patient lying still in a sterile bed beyond the wooden door, but a person with a name and a life she needed to live. If nothing else, perhaps he could offer her a sense that someone cared. He was a healer, and if that's what it took…

Sam knew it was an excuse to make himself feel better about wanting to be there. He didn't understand it but he felt some kind of bond with this young patient; no doubt one-sided since she'd been unconscious since shortly after the paramedics had brought her in. But perhaps in helping her, somehow he'd begin to heal. Heaven knew he needed it.

Laura's sudden proclamation she no longer loved him, that she was leaving and taking his girls had torn him apart. At 36, Sam was sure his life was over. And it was, in a sense. At least the life he'd known, expected to always be there. He'd thrown himself into his work and making the most of the two times a week he had to spend with his daughters, when work didn't detain him. He'd shut down to keep his heart from hurting and had done a pretty good job of not feeling until Emma Sanders had rolled into the ER on one of his rotation nights. 23 years old, a car wreck victim who looked more like she'd had the crap beaten out of her than she did someone who had tangled with metal and wood. And now she refused to wake up. There was something going on with her beyond whatever it was that had thoughts of her tugging at his heart and taking over his mind. She needed a reason to go on every bit as much as he did.

"Thanks, Wanda." Without waiting for a response from the older nurse, Sam pushed through the door to Emma's room. He froze as he stepped inside, his heart hammering while that little voice told him it was crazy to get involved in a stranger's life. Especially an unconscious stranger who had been his patient. He knew he should leave, even went so far as to reach for the door handle again. But he couldn't. She looked so … alone laying there, the bleeping of the monitors the only thing breaking the silence. Tomorrow, he would bring flowers and maybe balloons to liven up the room. Yes, that's what he'd do, he thought, nodding his head as he moved closer to her.

"Emma." It seemed peculiar to be calling her by her name. "I'm Dr. Walsh. Sam Walsh." He lowered his tall frame into the seat beside her bed and reached for her hand. "A colleague recommended a little game, a word game. I thought we'd give it a try," he fumbled, feeling funny. He decided not to mention the game was to help work the brain, get it firing, and hopefully help her wake up. Instead, he pulled out his phone, pulled up the words and began to read them and their definitions until he was too tired to go on.

Each afternoon Sam returned to Emma's room to play the word game, talk to her, and even read to her from a paperback they'd found among her belongings at the wreck site. It was the 6$^{th}$ day. No signs of waking. Sam was beginning to feel the strains of discouragement. He plopped down beside her bed. He was tired. Laura had been irritable when he called to check on the girls and make sure she remembered he was picking them up that evening for an overnight stay. It meant cutting his visit with Emma short, though he doubted she'd miss him much.

The thought made him chuckle, a low sound that rumbled through his chest and ended with a groan. He leaned forward, his head drooping, fingers pushing through his thick hair.

"Emma, Emma, Emma..." Sometimes he wished he could just go to sleep and block out the world for a while.

But he couldn't. He let out a long, loud exhale and pulled out his iPhone, pressing the buttons to get to the list of words. F-words. For some reason that made him laugh again. He was glad he had the next day off since it was pretty obvious he needed the break.

May as well get started, he thought. "Facile: Appearing neat and comprehensive by ignoring the complexities of an issue; superficial. Frenetic: Fast and energetic in a rather wild and uncontrolled way. Fastidious: Very attentive and concerned about accuracy and detail..." He sighed again. This wasn't working, at least for him.

Sam leaned over and grabbed Emma's book that remained exactly where he'd left it the day before. "Claire sat down on the edge of her bed to remove her shoes. She laid her phone on the nightstand next to the two waiting pill bottles then pulled off her earrings which she placed next to the phone. Putting a hand over her heart, she reached for the bottles with her empty hand and realized for the first time in a very long time she hadn't thought about the hurt inside for many hours. Maybe Garrett really was an angel. She considered the idea. Either way he'd altered the course of her life. She opened the nightstand drawer and dropped the bottles inside. A sudden wave of exhaustion engulfed her. Garrett was right. It was late. Claire looked at her phone and shook her head as she realized she hadn't gotten his number. Now the true question… was *he* a man of *his* word? Would he show on Sunday morning?"

Interesting how crossing paths with another can alter ones life. Sam put down the book, reached for Emma's hand and squeezed. "I don't know if I'll be here for the next couple of days, Emma. I have my rotation in the ER coming up and tomorrow I'll have my girls until late afternoon..."

Sam jumped, his eyes jerking down to look at their hands. She'd squeezed his hand. She had, hadn't she? His mind raced. What had he said? He wouldn't be there … ER rotation … day off … No! His girls.

"My… my girls are four and six." He laughed softly. "They're a handful…" There it was again. Yes! "Kimberly, Kimi, is the oldest. Has dark hair, full like mine only long and wavy. Sara looks more like her mom…"

Emma groaned a little. He felt more than saw her twisting beneath the sheets.

"I… I only get to see them a couple of times a week now…"

Her eyes fluttered several times then opened. He could tell she was unable to focus on him but he stood, smiling down at her just the same.

"Welcome back," he whispered, his free hand stroking the sandy tangles away from her face. She tried to return his smile though frowned instead before attempting to reach for the tube between her still-swollen lips. The loosely tied restraints, there for that very reason, checked her motion. Light blue eyes implored him to help her, just as they had right before she'd been taken into the operating room that night in the ER.

"It's okay. I'll get the nurse to see about getting that out." Without releasing her hand he pressed the button that would summons a nurse. He hoped it would be Wanda.

Sam had planned to leave after letting Emma know he'd be AWOL for a few days, even though he still had an hour and a half before time to pick up his girls. But her sudden awakening had been met with a flourish of activity and excitement. Sam knew he'd be even more exhausted when the adrenaline rush whooshed from his body. Hopefully he'd be home with the girls playing with some of their favorite toys in front of the fireplace. He smiled. Children were so resilient. They seemed to be adjusting better than the adults. His chest swelled knowing talk of his girls had been the catalyst to bring Emma back. She'd have to meet them…

"My baby?"

Her words cut through his thoughts like a dull sword. No one answered her, including him, even though he felt her eyes on him. His face contorted and he shook his head no after she mouthed *please*. She turned back to stare at the ceiling, a single tear welling in the corner of her eye, releasing to roll down the side of her face. That single tear broke his heart.

Emma didn't want to talk about why her parents never came to see her, refused to speak about the baby's father, or whether there had been any foul play prior to the accident. All of that leading Sam to believe more than ever there was something going on and that she needed someone by her side.

That, and the fact that he'd become quite attached to her during her hospital stay, brought about an offer that surprised them both. He didn't know where their relationship was headed, but he did have a spare bedroom in a big, lonely house where she was welcome to stay for as long as she needed. To his relief, Emma accepted the offer, though he realized on her part it may have been more out of having no place else to go. It didn't matter. He'd have her close by and that seemed to provide a healing they both needed and perhaps in time he'd have the opportunity to share with her the words that had begun to form in his heart; words that let him know the wounds inflicted by his own life were healing. Just like the woman in Emma's book, happenstance had changed his life. Opportunity knocked and he had, gratefully, opened the door to let her come inside.

Please consider joining my New Releases and Promo Information Only Newsletter. As the name implies, you will receive emails only when I have a new release or to inform you I have a promo going on (like free/99 cent books, or giveaways). And to thank you, I have a nearly 14,000 word story that's yours for free if you sign up. Currently, signing up is the only way to get *Makinna's Secret*, and you can find out more about it on my website.

Makinna Sharanis is the third child, the oldest daughter, and the only unmarried sibling of the Sharanis family. Her brothers are the infamous Tahruk and Redahn from my Romance Fantasy Series stories: *Dance With the Enemy* and *Beyond the Shadows*. Makinna and Rayles' story will take you further into the *Land of Riandus*, where the stories take place. It's a make believe land governed by some strange rules and a yearly moon that triggers events and makes things happen. It's a magical land with handsome warriors, beautiful women, kings and castles—all providing the backdrop for heartwarming, heat-provoking love stories.

# About Linda Boulanger

Linda Boulanger is a happily-ever-after author, wife, and mother of four human children and two fur babies. She has an eclectic mix of published books, numerous story singles and short stories in a few group anthologies, plus a slew of always evolving works in progress.

Along with being an author, she designs book covers for herself and others through *Tell~Tale Book Covers* and *TreasureLine Designs*, all from her desk just north of Tulsa, Oklahoma.

Other place to find Linda:

Website
http://www.LindaBoulangerBooks.com

Blog
http://writersshelflife.blogspot.com/

Facebook
https://www.facebook.com/TheShelfLifeOfLindaBoulanger

Email
lindaboulangerbooks@gmail.com

Amazon Author Page
http://www.amazon.com/Linda-Boulanger/e/B002NPYDC6

# Works by Linda Boulanger

**Novels/Novellas**
Dance With the Enemy
Beyond the Shadows
Arms of an Angel

**Mini-Novella**
Makinna's Secret
(this story is currently available free
with newsletter subscription only)

**Anthologies**
Echoed Heartbeats
Time Out on a Roller Coaster
Becoming...
Whispered Beginnings

**Color Illustrated Children's Book**
When Sadie Learned to S.M.I.L.E.

**Short Story Trios and Singles**
Up To Bat / Center Stage / Best Friend Rules
Face of an Angel / Life Changes / Talk With Me
Secret Shame

**Coming Soon/Works in Progress**
Temptation's Whisper (A Land of Riandus Novel)
Dark Warrior (Set in the Land of Riandus)
Marriage of Necessity (Contemporary Romance)
Selling Ellie (Contemporary Romance)

www.ingramcontent.com/pod-product-compliance
Lightning Source LLC
Chambersburg PA
CBHW060941120626

46557CB00003B/1094

* 9 7 8 1 6 1 7 5 2 0 3 7 2 *